DESERT SONG

Jeremiah knelt in the moist sand. He had just stuck his head in the stream when a bullet smacked the water a foot in front of his face. He leaped back, whirling toward the sound of the gunshot.

"Make yourself comfortable, piano player," Gordie Hodson said from the top of a small hill to Jeremiah's right, a revolver in his hand.

Jeremiah shot a glance at his own weapons, so near, yet so far away. A surge of fear made his skin turn hot and his body tremble.

"You going to shoot me down like you did my father?"

"Like father, like son," Gordie laughed. He raised the pistol and aimed it squarely at Jeremiah's chest.

JEREMIAH BACON

JAMES A. JANKE

A DELL BOOK

To Lily and Andy

CHAPTER ONE

Wednesday, June 15, 1880

Jeremiah Bacon rubbed his hands together to counter the night chill as he stepped down from the coach of the Union Pacific train. By the dim light emanating from the coach's windows, he could barely discern the large sign on the depot that said POINT OF ROCKS. Tugging at the bottom of his suit coat, he walked over to where another man, similarly attired, was standing with his arms akimbo, staring up at the sky.

"You don't suppose Wyoming really has more stars than Boston, do you, son?" the older man asked, seeing Jeremiah approach.

"No, Father," Jeremiah said, chuckling. He glanced up at the sea of twinkling dots that sparkled from horizon to horizon. "Odd how the city lights and buildings in Boston keep you from really seeing the sky," he said, appreciative of the view.

"Yes," Matthew Bacon agreed. He took a deep breath. "How about a walk down the street?" he suggested. "The conductor said we had about twenty minutes."

"Okay."

The two men crossed the short, dusty distance that separated the train station from the main street, which paralleled the tracks. They hesitated, debated their course, then headed to their right.

Matthew Bacon was tall and slim with nattily tailored clothes and a bowler. His erect posture and the carriage of his head, along with the touch of gray at his temples and in his carefully trimmed mustache and beard, gave him a decidedly distinguished appearance.

His son was twenty, exactly half his age. The young man was an inch taller than his father, carried himself in the same manner, and tended to copy his father's wardrobe, though his own light brown hair was unconfined by a hat. An observer, suspecting a familial relationship between the two men, would be convinced by the identical slight dimples in their respective chins.

Neither man spoke as they strolled, both preoccupied with the novelty of the small western town. The buildings were either adobe or wood frame, usually with a wooden boardwalk in front of each and sometimes an overhanging roof. The street was quiet; no pedestrians were about; there was no traffic and very few lights.

They passed a general store, a dress shop, a hardware store, and a meat market. They peered over the batwing doors of the Bitter Creek Saloon and noted a few quiet customers, several slouching in chairs at tables, one propped up at the bar. A bored saloon girl in a red dress sauntered from one table to another; the bartender stood behind the bar, staring into space, slowly wiping a glass.

A dry goods store was next, then a saddlery, a furniture store, and a lawyer's office. Jeremiah and his father crossed the street and reversed directions, stopping to look at a single horse standing in the corral attached to a livery stable. A barbershop separated the livery from the marshal's office and jail. City Hall was singularly unimpressive. A bank followed, then a confectioner's, a dry goods store, a restaurant, a gunsmith, and a bakery. More shops and offices, some empty, each striking the two men as crude and quaint compared to the vast edifices of the big eastern cities.

"Isn't it about time we got back, Father?" Jeremiah asked apprehensively, glancing back at the station, which they'd passed again.

"Oh, let's see," the older man said, pulling a gold watch from his pocket. With a click the cover popped open, but turn the watch as he might, Matthew Bacon could not read the time in the darkness. He looked about.

"Ah," he said, "there seems to be a light in this Wells Fargo office." He stepped up to a window and held the watch up to a sliver of light that crept around the edge of a shade. "Another five minutes," he announced. "Perhaps we should return."

He snapped the cover of the watch shut and inserted the timepiece into his pocket, casually peering into the office past the ill-fitting shade as he did so. Jeremiah noticed him suddenly freeze and then investigate more closely.

"Why—men with guns!" Matthew said, astonished.

"What?" Jeremiah asked. He started for the window himself.

"Yes," his father confirmed. "They seem to be pointing it at— Oh, my God!"

"What's wrong?" Jeremiah asked anxiously.

His father motioned him back. "They heard me," he gasped. "Get back!"

Jeremiah stood transfixed to the spot.

"Run, for God's sake!" Matthew commanded, pushing Jeremiah. Jeremiah turned and started running; his father was right behind him.

The door of the office rattled and then opened, banging up against the inside wall. Two men burst out and fell upon the Bacons before they were even away from the office.

"Run, Jeremiah!" Matthew shouted. He grappled with both the assailants, preventing them from reaching Jeremiah.

Jeremiah continued running. He looked back and saw his father being dragged inside the office as yet another figure darted out. The man pointed toward Jeremiah; a light flashed, and a bullet whizzed past Jeremiah's head just as he heard a loud bang. Jeremiah ducked between two buildings.

"Dammit, missed," Jeremiah heard the gunman

snarl in a peculiar gravelly voice. "You two, after 'im," the man commanded. Two men started a chase.

Jeremiah felt his scalp crawl, and a surge of fear swept his body. He could hear the pursuers coming, the rapid clumping of their boots on the boardwalk like a drum roll at an execution. He ran wildly, one foot barely touching the ground before he was off on another bound.

Jeremiah was at a distinct disadvantage. The only other people around that he knew of were at the train station and the saloon—both in the opposite direction. The layout of the town was unfamiliar to him, but his pursuers could very well be residents.

He raced along the side of a building, his hands pushing off its surface as he plunged blindly toward the unknown area in the darkness ahead. He dodged between other buildings, ran through some scraggly bushes, and cut across yards. His legs pumped feverishly, his heart pounded so hard he thought it would tie itself into a knot, his lungs sucked air in short, wheezing gasps that clawed at his throat.

He saw a home that showed a light in the window, and he ran for that, hoping he'd be able to rouse its occupants. But as he reached the porch, he caught sight of the two men chasing him. If he raised the alarm they would shoot him down at the door. But he was exhausted; he could run no farther.

Jeremiah threw himself desperately among some bushes that grew alongside the house. He lay there gasping for air. The two pursuers came running up, one darting along the short picket fence that bordered part of the yard, the other stalking up to the lighted window. Jeremiah held his breath. Panting heavily, the man cautiously peered into the window.

"Is he there?" the man along the fence whispered.

"Nah," the man at the window answered disgustedly. With the barrel of his pistol he pushed the tip of his hat back, and Jeremiah saw his face in the illumination. It was gaunt and oval-shaped, with a ragged black mustache and a couple of days' growth of beard. "Could've sworn I saw him come this way," the robber said. He looked around anxiously, searching the shadows.

"I don't like this," the other man complained. "That shot must've roused somebody."

"I don't like it either," the man at the window agreed. "Hell, Tom, let's get outa here."

"I'm for that." The two men ran from the yard and headed back toward the Wells Fargo office.

Thinking only of the danger his father must be in, Jeremiah forgot the probable safety of the house and hurried after the outlaws, keeping under cover. He soon found himself near the back of the Wells Fargo office, crouching apprehensively behind a barrel outside an adjacent building. He was torn between staying near his father and going for help.

A muffled report, followed quickly by two others, broke into Jeremiah's thoughts. He realized they must have been gunshots, and the thought made him nauseous. He started to tremble. The back door of the office opened, and four men rushed out, ran to four horses tethered near the door, and threw themselves into their saddles.

Jeremiah shrank back farther into the shadows, and his frightened eyes followed the galloping animals through the choking dust raised by their hooves. One horse, a striking black with white stockings, stood out against the plain brown of the others.

Boots slapped against the flanks of horses, bridles clicked, and saddle leather creaked and complained as the men urged their mounts onward. With a heavy pounding of hooves, the four horsemen were quickly out of sight, and quiet returned.

Jeremiah bolted from behind the barrel and ran with fear to the back door of the Wells Fargo office. He plunged into the dark interior of the building and fumbled his way down a hall, using his hands for eyes. There were obviously several rooms to the building, but it was not long before Jeremiah was in the front office.

He shuddered. In the faint glow from the windows Jeremiah could make out the vague forms of two bodies, one crumpled up against the counter in the office, the other spread-eagled on the floor near the door.

He knelt by the nearest body, his lips trembling, and he whispered a soft, "Father?" His hands explored the face of the man, a full-fleshed face, with no beard. It was not Matthew Bacon. Jeremiah heard gurgling sounds escape the man's throat.

Jeremiah crept on his hands and knees over to the supine figure that he knew had to be his father. With a trembling hand he reached for the man's face, and the facial hair he touched confirmed his worst fears. "Oh, my God!" he gasped. "Father!" His fingers sought the man's jugular vein, but there was no sign of a pulse. Jeremiah ran his hand gently down his father's chest. "Father, Father," he sobbed, fighting back tears.

He froze, sucking in his breath as his hand slipped through a warm fluid that had collected on the vest of Matthew Bacon. Jeremiah raised his hand and felt its palm with the other hand. "Oh, Jesus in heaven," he said in anguish.

He rose to his feet and reached into his pocket to remove his handkerchief. Grimacing, he wiped the blood off his hand and then stepped gingerly over his father's body and headed for the front door. He fumbled for the doorknob, then threw the door wide open. He rushed out onto the boardwalk and paused at the edge.

"Help," he said feebly, the lump in his throat choking off his voice. Then he gathered his strength and screamed, "Help! Murder!" He ran into the street. "Help!"

Jeremiah saw a man running his way, the tails of an unbuttoned shirt flapping behind him, a holster held in his left hand, and a pistol in his right. Jeremiah ran to meet him.

"I heard shots," the man said. "What's happened?"

"Help me," Jeremiah pleaded, grabbing the man's right arm.

The man jerked his arm away. "Let go of my gun hand, you idiot," he scolded.

Jeremiah was startled by the rebuff. He stared at the man, trying to formulate a reply. "My father," he said, pleading. He jerked his thumb in the direction of the Wells Fargo office.

The other man's tone softened. "Show me," he said simply. He nudged Jeremiah's shoulder with the flat of his pistol.

"Over here," Jeremiah said, and he turned and ran for the office, glancing back to make sure the man continued to trot after him. Jeremiah ran into the office and knelt down by his father, picking up a still hand in his own.

The other man ran up to the office door, but he hid behind the door frame and peered into the dark office.

"In here," Jeremiah insisted.

"I didn't get to be forty-three in my job by rushing blindly into dark buildings, mister," the man said.

"Oh," Jeremiah replied. "Uh—they left," he said. "Four of them—on horses they had in back."

Finally the man entered and knelt down on the other side of Matthew Bacon's body.

"He's been shot," Jeremiah said. "He's hurt bad," he continued, refusing to believe the worst.

The other man felt for life signs, then took a deep breath and gave a sigh. "I'm sorry," he said. "Your father's dead."

Dead! That couldn't be, it just couldn't be! They were just walking down the street together. Just talking with each other. It was just not possible. Jeremiah clutched his father's hand in both of his, holding it close to his chest. "Oh merciful God," he pleaded.

A murmur came from the wounded man lying near the counter.

"Who's that?"

"I don't know," Jeremiah answered. "They shot him along with—" He couldn't finish.

"Could use some light in here," the man said, rising to his feet. Jeremiah heard the gun being slipped into its holster, the slap of the leather against a hip, and the click of a buckle. The man walked to the side of the room and then stopped. A burst of light lit up the room as a match hissed into flame. He turned around. "Oh, Jesus," he said.

Jeremiah saw what the man really looked like for the first time. A large barrel-chested man, with huge hands. His head was square shaped, topped by a disheveled crop of brown hair that lapped his collar. He had a broad nose and slightly bushy eyebrows and sideburns. Jeremiah had never seen a countenance that conveyed authority like this man's did. He was not surprised to see the star-shaped badge on the man's shirt.

"Cyrus," the lawman said, kneeling down. "It's me, Otis MacKenzie."

The man on the floor tried to speak, but only pitiful gasps and groans issued from his mouth.

"Did you see them, Cyrus?" the marshal asked. "Did you recognize any of them?"

"Cow—"

"Cowhand?" Otis said. "One of them was a cowhand?"

"Ye—"

"What ranch was he from, Cyrus?"

There was no answer.

"Cyrus?" MacKenzie checked for a pulse, then a heartbeat. He patted the dead man's shoulder. "So long, Cyrus, old friend."

A woman screamed in the office. Otis whirled and saw a woman in a long traveling coat standing in the doorway, her hands to the side of her head, horror on her face.

"Mother," Jeremiah said in anguish, looking up at her.

Priscilla Bacon screamed her husband's name and sank to her knees at his side. Her hands floated over his body, desperately wanting to touch him, but repulsed by the ugly red stain on his chest. Then she broke into deep, body-shaking sobs and flung herself on the man, cradling his head in her hands.

"Mother," Jeremiah repeated softly. He put his hands on her shaking shoulders, but he felt absolutely helpless. He looked up at the marshal beseechingly. The lawman, busily tucking his buttoned shirt into his pants, seemed equally at a loss.

Otis went out the door and spoke to the gawking spectators who had gathered, sending first one and then another off on errands. He turned back to the Bacon family, but he realized there was nothing he could do. While he waited, he made a cursory inspection of the open safe in the office and noted that its contents had been removed.

A portly woman in a simple cotton dress and shawl waddled with much huffing and puffing into the Wells Fargo office.

"Mrs. Munford," the marshal said, greeting her. "Could you be of some assistance here?" he asked. But the question was unnecessary. Thelma Munford had been raised on the frontier and had seen much of her family, including her parents and husband, and neighbors, struck down by Indians, outlaws, starvation, and disease. Familiarity with tragedy breeds only acceptance, not insensitivity. She knelt down beside the prostrate widow and put a comforting hand on her shoulder, saying nothing, for nothing could be said.

A wagon drew up in front of the office. The crowd parted, and a man entered reverently. "Marshal," he said simply.

Mrs. Munford saw the man enter, and she spoke

to Priscilla Bacon. "My dear," she said, starting to lift the other woman away. "They've come for your husband."

"No, no," Priscilla refused.

"Life is hard," Mrs. Munford soothed. "We must accept these things. We don't have to understand them or like them, but we have to accept them. Come," she repeated, pulling more forcefully, "let the men do their duty."

Jeremiah stood up and glanced at the man who had entered.

"Taylor Pierce," the marshal explained. "Town undertaker. He'll see to your father."

Jeremiah nodded. He returned to his mother and helped Mrs. Munford get her to her feet.

"Cry your heart out, dear," Mrs. Munford said, enfolding the much smaller woman in her great arms. "It helps the soul."

Pierce crooked a finger at several men in the doorway. Quickly and silently they came in, picked up the body of Cyrus, and carried it out to the wagon. Just as quickly they returned and did the same with the body of Matthew Bacon. The undertaker tipped his hat solemnly to Jeremiah and left.

"Mrs. Munford," Otis said, "could these people stay with you for the night? They're in mighty great need of comfortin'."

"Of course, Marshal," she agreed. "Come along—" She paused. "What's the poor woman's name, Marshal?"

"Priscilla Bacon, m'am," Jeremiah volunteered. He turned to the marshal. "My name is Jeremiah Bacon. My father is—Matthew Bacon."

"Come, Priscilla," Mrs. Munford said, leading her out of the office. "You'll stay at my home." The two women left the office and proceeded down the boardwalk, Priscilla murmuring protests, but helpless in her grief.

"You must've come in on the train," Otis said t Jeremiah.

"Yes, sir," Jeremiah confirmed. "My father and I went for a walk," he explained in a muted voice. "He saw the men in this office and they saw him. They came out, seized him, and chased me. I eluded the ones chasing me and came back here. I heard shots. The men rode away and I ran in and found—" He waved his hand over the floor. In the distance he could still faintly hear the clopping of the horse's hooves and the creaking of the wagon.

"What'd they look like?"

"I only saw one man's face. Kind of oblong, thin. He had black hair and a mustache. Rather short, too."

"Doesn't help a whole lot," the marshal said, rubbing his chin. "Could be one of a number of fellows, I'm afraid."

"I'd recognize him if I saw him again," Jeremiah said firmly. "Oh, he called one of the other men 'Tom.'"

"Tom? Pretty common name, but it's more than we had before. Anything else?"

"The leader had a peculiar voice, sort of gruff, forced, scratchy."

"Voices are pretty hard to recognize from someone else's description," Otis commented, "but it sounds like a description I've heard before."

"One of the horses was black with white feet," Jeremiah added.

"That's not a real common type, might be real helpful. Anything else?"

Jeremiah shook his head.

"Well," Otis said, sighing. "It's too dark to track 'em now. I'll get a posse and start after 'em at first light. 'Bout five hours from now."

Jeremiah nodded.

"You ought to go be near your mother, son," the marshal suggested. "Did you have any baggage?"

"Yes, sir."

"I'll have it taken off the train and sent to Mrs. Munford's."

"Thank you."

CHAPTER TWO

Thursday, June 16, 1880

Otis MacKenzie took off his hat and beat it against his pants to remove as much of the dust as possible. He stepped onto the porch of Mrs. Munford's small white-frame home on the northern edge of town, near the gray sandstone cliffs that bordered Point of Rocks. The silence struck him. Mrs. Munford had apparently shooed her three kids, the last of eight still at home, off to somewhere else to allow the Bacons some peace and quiet.

Mrs. Munford received him at the door and led him into the parlor, where Priscilla and Jeremiah were both sitting. Then she returned to the kitchen.

Somewhat awkwardly the marshal stood in front of the two people. "I'm sorry," he said. "We followed their trail clear up to Emmons Cone, but they scattered there. We split up, too, but each of the trails disappeared. We lost 'em."

"You've done all you could, Marshal," Priscilla Bacon said softly. "We thank you. Please sit down." She motioned with a hand.

The marshal sat down in an easy chair. "There's always the chance that the men may still be caught, m'am," he said. He studied the widow, not having remembered much about her from the previous night. Fine features on her oval-shaped face, her light-brown hair tied back in a bun. A dainty, rounded nose over perfectly proportioned lips that revealed a set of even white teeth when they parted. Slim, yet full figured.

A comely woman, indeed. Her eyes seemed the more tragic for it, since she'd obviously been crying a great deal.

"Yes," the woman commented. "Mrs. Munford mentioned that the men were probably members of the Red Desert Gang, as she called them."

"That's right, m'am," the marshal agreed. "And they seem to stick around this area, have for a number of years, so there's a good chance we'll run into 'em again and catch the murderers."

"I dearly hope so, Marshal," she said. "By the way, we have another clue that may help you. In preparing my husband for burial we discovered that his watch was gone. His murderers must have taken it."

"What did it look like?"

"It was gold. I gave it to him on our wedding day. The date is inscribed on the cover—June second, eighteen fifty-eight."

"Good, I'll keep an eye out for it."

"Mrs. Munford said the other man murdered was the Wells Fargo agent," Priscilla stated.

"Yes, m'am."

"What was he doing there at that time of night?"

"A shipment of greenbacks and coins had come in on the train Tuesday. It was scheduled to go up to Atlantic City on today's stage, to be exchanged for gold dust and bullion from the mines. The agent was staying at the office overnight to guard the shipment; he did that often."

"Why weren't you guarding it?" Jeremiah asked, speaking for the first time.

"That was his job," Otis said, sensing an implied accusation of dereliction of duty. "Besides, Cyrus Kessler was as capable of defendin' that money as I would've been. He spent eighteen years in the cavalry, went through some of the fiercest fightin' in the War Between the States and then spent a decade fightin' Indians before he quit and took the job here. He was as handy with a gun as I am and probably twice as tough in a fight."

"I'm surprised a man of action like that would have taken so sedentary a position as that of a Wells Fargo agent," Priscilla commented.

"It was his wife' m'am," he explained. "She tired of the army life, wanted to settle down. So—"

"Mrs. Munford said that Mr. Kessler was a widower," Priscilla said, puzzled.

"Yes, m'am. His wife was killed soon after they got to Point of Rocks."

"Oh—an awful shame."

Otis noted that she said it with genuine sympathy, not as a polite, reflexive response.

"This must all be very hard for the daughter," Priscilla judged. "Anita, I believe Mrs. Munford said."

"Yes, m'am," the marshal said. "Anita Kessler."

"Will you see her today?"

"Yes, I believe I will."

"Please extend our sympathy to her, the poor child," Priscilla said.

"I sure will, m'am," Otis agreed. "She'll appreciate the gesture."

There was a lull in the conversation. "Uh—I suppose you'll be leavin' soon after the funeral tomorrow," Otis said, trying to make conversation.

"No," Jeremiah said firmly.

"No?" the marshal asked, surprised.

"Not until my father's murderers are brought to justice," Jeremiah vowed.

"Well," Otis said, glancing uncomfortably at Priscilla. "That could be some time, m'am," he said awkwardly.

"We're staying," Jeremiah reaffirmed.

Priscilla patted his hand lovingly. "Now, now, Jeremiah," she chided. She turned again to the lawman. "Actually, Marshal MacKenzie, I am inclined to agree with my son, temporarily at least. You see, we were heading for San Francisco, where Matthew had secured a position at the symphony and at the University of California in Oakland. He was a superb violinist."

"I see."

"Now there is no reason for us to continue on to San Francisco or to return to Boston."

"Surely there is some family, some friends."

"There is no family, and we would be imposing on friends. More importantly, tomorrow my heart will be planted in Point of Rocks along with the body of my husband. I find it difficult myself to consider leaving, at least for a while."

"But how will you get along?" Otis asked. "I don't mean to pry, but have you any money?"

"An item which we have in short supply, I'm afraid, sir," she admitted. "It will be necessary for me to find gainful employment."

Otis glanced at the healthy young man at her side. "Seems to me, m'am," he suggested, "that the boy there should be the one lookin' for a job."

"I intend to find work, Marshal," Jeremiah said hastily.

"Marshal MacKenzie," Priscilla broke in, noting the increasingly belligerent tone in both men's voices. "I must explain. Jeremiah," she said, grasping her son's hands, "has a rare talent for the piano. He plans on becoming a concert pianist. My husband's position would have allowed Jeremiah to enter the College of Fine Arts at the University this fall term. Now that seems improbable, but I will devote my life to see that his ambition is still achieved, that his plans for further education are realized as soon as possible. Of course, for now it will be necessary for him to work, also," she conceded, "but any employment that he might find must be strictly temporary and not injurious to his hands."

Otis raised an eyebrow.

"Mother," Jeremiah said, somewhat embarrassed in

front of the rugged man sitting across from them. "I'll have to take what work I can find. The piano must be of secondary importance until Father's murderers are found."

"Oh, shush, Jeremiah," his mother scolded. "I'll not hear of your abandoning the piano. Your father's death must not also be the demise of your future."

Otis liked the way Priscilla Bacon talked. She was obviously educated, yet she did not flaunt her education. She wasn't trying to be a snob; that was simply the way she talked.

"No, Jeremiah," his mother said. "These hands were made for great things." She squeezed his hands. "I'll do whatever is necessary, here in Point of Rocks and later in San Francisco, to see them fulfill their destiny. I'd be so proud, and so would your father." She looked admiringly at her son.

Otis was deeply impressed. Pride, dignity, intelligence, manners, devotion, compassion—she had it all. He searched for a word for what she had. Class. That was it. She had class.

"Well," he said, "I speak for the whole town when I say you are both welcome here. And you'll find the people helpful and friendly."

"Thank you, Marshal," she said.

"Well," Otis said, "I've got to be goin'." He rose and started to back away.

"Marshal MacKenzie," Jeremiah addressed him.

"Yes?" Otis stopped.

"If the Red Desert Gang has been operating in this area for several years, why haven't you caught its members by now?" The displeasure in his voice was unmistakable.

"Now just a minute—" Otis said, raising a finger. He felt on the defensive again.

"Jeremiah," Priscilla virtually snapped. "You are being rude and unfair. I'm sure the marshal has done all he could."

Jeremiah thought over the last night. How his grief

had crushed him, a heavy pressure on his chest, a hollowness in his stomach, an aching in his throat and head. And then it had been supplanted by a new emotion, an emotion he hadn't realized he could feel with such intensity. Anger. Anger and hate. Whereas the piano had been his only interest up until now, henceforth he would be ruled by a new passion—vengeance.

"I want them dead," Jeremiah said sternly. "I want them caught and executed."

"You're not alone in that desire, Mr. Bacon," Otis readily agreed, irritated.

"You can depend on me for any help you need, Marshal," Jeremiah offered, "but if you can't do the job I'll do it myself. And I'll have no mercy for them."

"Nor they for you," Otis warned. His resentment turned to pity suddenly. How many times had he seen fiery young men turn themselves into righteous avengers, only to end up maimed or dead. But he understood the young man's anger. "You'll only get yourself hurt—or killed," he said sympathetically. "Let me handle it."

"Of course he will, Marshal," Priscilla said, alarmed. "Jeremiah, I'll not tolerate any such talk on your part."

Jeremiah fell silent and sullen.

Otis started to back up again, unsure how to break off the conversation, which had turned decidedly unpleasant. "Mrs. Bacon," he said simply, nodding. "Mr. Bacon."

"Thank you for stopping by, Marshal," Priscilla replied graciously.

CHAPTER THREE

Friday, June 17, 1880

The sun beat straight down as the large group of somber figures clustered around the two gravesites in the cemetery outside of Point of Rocks.

"We are gathered here to lay to rest the remains of two beloved brethren," the Reverend Crockett said. "Two good men cut down in the prime of life by cold-blooded assassins. Evil people so in love with the material wealth of this world that they would destroy the real wealth of the world—its good people."

Jeremiah listened absently to the man speak. He was staring at the simple wooden box that lay on the ground next to the heap of dirt that had been scooped out of the earth. Incredible that his father, having been a warm, loving human being just two days earlier, should be lying in that box.

". . . a loving wife . . ." Jeremiah glanced up at his mother who stood beside him. She wore the same blue dress in which she had arrived in Point of Rocks, but a large black shawl covered her shoulders. Her head was bowed, her eyes closed, a tear on each cheek. She held a Bible close to her bosom, grasping it so tightly that her knuckles were white.

". . . a devoted daughter . . ." On the other side of the two graves stood Anita Kessler, a young woman, dressed in black, her head bowed, heavily veiled, her hands folded in front of her.

Jeremiah also noted the young man standing close to her, a deputy marshal's badge affixed to his vest. He was tall and lean, with black hair and a wispy mustache on a lip overhung by a pointed nose that seemed to reach for an equally jutting chin. He had a heavy shadow to his face, and thick black hair swept from under his shirt-sleeves to flow over his hands and fingers, which had rolled up the brim of the hat held in front of him.

". . . brought to swift justice . . ." Jeremiah glanced over at Otis MacKenzie, who shifted his feet, apparently aware of Jeremiah's accusing stare.

". . . ashes to ashes, dust to dust . . ." Jeremiah pondered the transitory nature of a man's life.

". . . I shall not want. He maketh me to lie down in green pastures. He restoreth . . ." His father was at peace, but Jeremiah was certain *he* could never be at peace with himself until the murderers of his father were also dead.

"Amen." The minister nodded toward the crowd, and four men came forward. They picked up the ends of two pieces of rope on which the coffin of Matthew Bacon lay and lifted the box into the air. Straining in the heat, they maneuvered the box over the open grave and then started lowering it slowly, letting it pass out of sight.

Jeremiah was startled as his mother started singing.

> "All men living are but mortal,
> Yea, all flesh must fade as grass,
> Only thro' death's gloomy portal
> To eternal life we pass."

The men with the ropes stopped the descent and looked up at the minister, fearful they'd made a mistake. The minister, equally confused, looked first at Priscilla and then at the men again. He motioned for them to continue.

Jeremiah looked at his mother in surprise. Her eyes were still closed, and her head swayed slowly from side to side. Her voice cracked in the beginning, but it picked up strength as she went on. His father had always been proud of his wife's singing, and Jeremiah saw this as his mother's parting tribute to her husband.

> "The frail body here must perish
> Ere the heav'nly joys it cherish,
> Ere it gain the free reward
> For the ransomed of the Lord."

The lump in Jeremiah's throat felt like it would break through the walls of his neck. Never had he heard such heart-rending singing. He looked around the crowd. All eyes were on Priscilla, even those of Anita Kessler. Several women dabbed at their eyes, and Jeremiah even noticed the marshal blink rapidly several times.

The men finished lowering the coffin into the grave, and two of them dropped their ends of the ropes while the other two pulled up briskly. Quickly they went to the other coffin, and soon it too sank out of sight. The box thudded softly as it touched the bottom of the hole. Again ropes were withdrawn, the rasping of the fiber on the edges of the coffin echoing in the cavity with a grim finality.

> "Thus before the throne so glorious,
> Now ye stand a soul victorious,
> Gazing on that joy for aye,
> That shall never pass away.
> Amen."

Priscilla's voice finished strong now, clear and crisp. The crowd was motionless. Jeremiah could taste a salty liquid as it trickled into the side of his mouth, and he unobtrusively wiped away the tears with the back of his hand.

"Jeremiah," his mother said, "your arm, please."

"Yes, Mother," he said, quickly extending his arm for her to hold. They started down the dusty path that led to the town, and the rest of the crowd began dispersing as well. From back at the gravesite Jeremiah heard the chink of shovels as they bit into the mounds of dirt, and then he heard the hollow-sounding *thunk* as each shovelful hit the wooden lids of the coffins.

"The Lord giveth, and the Lord taketh away," Reverend Crockett said to Mrs. Munford as the two of them watched Priscilla and Jeremiah descend the path. "But the agony and pathos in that woman's voice must have given Him second thoughts."

"Yes, Reverend," Mrs. Munford said. "An angel, an angel." She blew her nose gently. "You will come by the house, won't you?" she asked. "Both families will be there."

"Of course, Mrs. Munford," he assured her. "Of course."

The people at Mrs. Munford's stood in small groups, talking softly over coffee and sandwiches. Everyone expressed their sympathy to Anita and to the Bacons, even though they didn't know the latter.

Mrs. Munford introduced Anita Kessler to Jeremiah and his mother. Jeremiah was immediately taken by the young woman. Her black hair formed a frame of tight curls about a round face with cheeks that had a natural, fresh rosiness to them and with large, dark-brown eyes. She had a short, rounded nose and an unusually wide mouth that enhanced the allure of her lovely lips. The somber black dress did not detract in the least from her fine figure.

The three people, though strangers, talked easily, for they had suffered a common calamity, and it had instantly forged a bond between them. They were engaged in a subdued conversation when Marshal MacKenzie approached them, his huge right hand encompassing a coffee cup, from which he sipped occasionally

After they had accepted his renewed words of sym

pathy, Anita Kessler informed him of the new accommodations for Priscilla.

"Priscilla has accepted my invitation to come live with me, as you suggested, Marshal," she said.

"Splendid," he replied. "I'm sure the two of you will be good company for each other. Mrs. Munford would love to have you here, Mrs. Bacon, but a house full of kids might not be the best for you."

"I'm very grateful for Anita's offer," Priscilla said, "and I'm sure we will get along fine. However, there is still the matter of a living place for Jeremiah."

"Oh, well, I thought he could stay at the jail," Otis suggested.

"The jail!" Priscilla exclaimed, astonished.

"Oh, a temporary arrangement until something more suitable comes along," he quickly added.

"Would I sleep in a cell?" Jeremiah asked.

"Yes, but the door would be left open." He looked at Priscilla. "No one would think he was under arrest or anything," he assured the concerned woman.

"Still, sleeping in a jail," she said skeptically.

"It might be interesting, Mother," Jeremiah volunteered.

"M'am," the marshal argued, "*I* sleep there."

"Well," she said, distressed at having offended the lawman, "I guess it's satisfactory. As long as it's temporary."

"Of course," Otis acknowledged.

"I can bring my things over later today, Marshal," Jeremiah said.

"Fine." The marshal shifted the cup to his other hand. "I've also thought of a possible job for you, son."

"Oh?" both Priscilla and Jeremiah said.

"Yes, and it allows you to keep practicing the piano."

"That's wonderful, Marshal," Priscilla said excitedly.

"Well, the Bitter Creek Saloon needs a piano player for nights—"

"What!" Priscilla exclaimed. "My son playing piano in a—a saloon. Really, Marshal, it's too much."

Otis was taken aback. "It's honest work, m'am. And the saloon has the only piano in town."

"That's right, Priscilla," Anita confirmed.

"Oh, but really," Priscilla scoffed.

"It can't be so bad, Mother," Jeremiah said. "It will provide some money, and the piano is important."

"If your father could see you—" She paused, weighing the matter. "You have us at a disadvantage, Marshal MacKenzie."

"Yes, m'am," he allowed.

"I'll take the job, Marshal," Jeremiah announced.

His mother did not protest, resigned to the situation. "But it's only temporary, until more appropriate employment is found," she set as a condition.

"Of course," Otis agreed. "I'll take you over to the saloon about nine tonight," he said to Jeremiah.

"Good," the young man returned. "I'll be ready."

Otis smiled at the three people. Anita Kessler. How proud Cyrus had been of her. Capable, she ran the agency probably more than he had. And pretty and charming. No wonder his deputy as well as most of the other young men in the Sweetwater region were chasing her. Priscilla Bacon. The first woman he'd ever met that he felt awed by. Something really extraordinary about her. And that singing. Nothing had ever touched him as much as that had. Jeremiah Bacon. He liked the way the young man stood, straight-shouldered, erect, proud. And he didn't turn away if you looked him straight in the eye. But also headstrong and impulsive and likely to get himself killed if he was allowed to pursue his quest for vengeance. A potential tragedy and additional blow to his mother.

"Well," Otis said, finishing the last sip of the coffee.

"I have some things to do. I'll be talkin' to each of you."

The trio said good-bye to the marshal, and he left the group, to be replaced immediately by three other men.

"Anita," the spokesman said, "our deepest sympathy. You know how we loved your father."

"Thank you, gentlemen," Anita said.

"And would you introduce us to the Bacons, please," he added.

Anita nodded. "Mrs. Priscilla Bacon and her son, Jeremiah," she began. "This is Mr. Henkleman, owner of the Point of Rocks general store and mayor of the city."

"My sympathy to both of you," Henkleman said.

"Thank you," Priscilla said. Jeremiah nodded.

"This is Mr. Osborne," Anita continued. "He's owner of the local bank and chairman of the school board." Osborne extended his condolences. "And the Reverend Crockett you already know," Anita said, finishing the introductions.

"Of course," Priscilla acknowledged. "Thank you for the kind words at the funeral, Reverend."

"I hope I was able to give you some comfort."

"You did. Thank you."

"Mrs. Bacon," Henkleman said. "The marshal has informed us that you intend to stay in Point of Rocks for a while, is that correct?"

"Yes, it is."

"And he also mentioned that you would be seeking employment."

"Yes," Priscilla repeated.

"The marshal suggested that you were an educated lady?" Osborne asked, seeking confirmation.

"I have had a year of college," Priscilla stated.

"Fine," Osborne said. "Well, Point of Rocks needs a teacher for its children for the fall, and we would like to offer the position to you."

"Why, I'm flattered, gentlemen," Priscilla said, taken aback.

"Mother," Jeremiah encouraged, "you've always been interested in teaching."

"You'll accept the offer?" Osborne asked.

Priscilla debated, then decided quickly. "I accept."

"Good, good," Osborne said, nodding.

"Of course," Henkleman interjected, "school doesn't start until fall. However, I could use someone to help me with the bookkeeping and accounts in the store. Are you good with figures, Mrs. Bacon?"

"I'd say I have a fairly good command of the subject, Mr. Henkleman," she said confidently. "I'm sure I could handle it—with a little help in the beginning."

"You may start whenever you like," the man said.

"Thank you, thank you all," Priscilla said gratefully. "You have eased my mind a considerable amount. I—I am simply overwhelmed by the generosity and by the concern everyone is showing for us, by your help, your offers."

Reverend Crockett spoke up. "I, also, would like to make an offer," he said, "but mine comes without monetary remuneration. However, I think you could find it profitable nonetheless."

"Oh?" she asked, curious.

"The Good Book," the minister said, remembering Priscilla's Bible, "is a great comfort, but even more comforting is being with people who care for you and who can share your burden of sorrow. I speak for the entire congregation when I ask the two of you to join us in worship on Sunday and on every Sunday."

"We'd love to have you come," Anita put in.

"Of course, we'll be there," Priscilla said. "And thank you for inviting us."

"And—well—" the minister said haltingly, "could we impose upon you to sing at the service for us?"

"Me?"

"Your voice, madam," he gushed, "the depths of feeling, the expression of the soul, the fineness of the voice—a hymn of your choice, naturally."

Priscilla smiled. "I'd be honored to sing at your service," she said.

"It is we who are honored. And God bless you."

The three men expressed their sympathy once more and then departed.

"Mother," Jeremiah said slowly, "I am amazed at the number of nice people there are in this town."

"I quite agree, son," Priscilla said. She turned to Anita. "I am deeply touched by the way so many people have rushed to the assistance of two perfect strangers."

Anita smiled. "You won't be strangers long," she said.

CHAPTER FOUR

Friday, June 17, 1880

At ten to nine in the evening Otis MacKenzie swung the batwing doors of the Bitter Creek Saloon wide with a push of his big hands and strode purposefully into the smokey interior. Jeremiah followed him somewhat timidly, hanging close to the man.

"You wait here, Bacon," Otis said. "I want to talk to Zwieg first."

"Yes, sir," Jeremiah acknowledged. Otis headed for an office door in the back of the saloon, and Jeremiah started a close scrutiny of the place, it being the first saloon he'd ever been in.

The establishment was wide with a high ceiling. Along the left side of the room stretched a long bar with a foot-rail at the bottom and a spittoon at each end and one in the middle. Back of the bar were many shelves well-stocked with bottles and small kegs. A large mirror also occupied much of the wall behind the bar, and above the mirror hung a large oil painting of a reclining nude woman.

At the back of the saloon, next to the door through which the marshal had disappeared, a hallway led farther back into the building, leading to another door that apparently opened to the outside. A stairway at the right in the back of the building led up to a balcony, which, in turn, led to another hallway, directly over the one below.

Under the stairway and extending about eight feet into the room was a small elevated stage, perhaps two feet off the level of the floor. Pushed up against the stage and abutting the railing of the stairway was an upright piano.

The rest of the saloon was filled with round tables about which four or five chairs were commonly grouped. The right-hand wall was largely blank with a single window set in the midst of some faded, peeling wallpaper that contrasted with the wooden wainscot that encircled the entire room. Lamps hung from the walls and ceiling, and there were several potbellied stoves scattered along the walls, winter being no deterrent to the saloon's business.

The bar was one-third lined with men, and nearly every table had at least someone at it, a few tables being full. Poker games were in progress, some men just sat and talked while they drank, and at one table a lone man repeatedly filled a glass from a nearly empty bottle and drank its contents down with a toss of his head.

Two saloon girls wandered about, laughing and giggling and coyly slipping out of someone's grasp or into a lap if the owner ordered a bottle from the bar. Both girls wore lowcut dresses with high-heeled shoes and gaudy but frayed feathers tucked in their hair, the feathers dyed to match the faded colors of the dresses, one yellow and the other red. The girl in yellow was plain and rather hefty, but the other one was quite striking.

Suddenly Jeremiah caught the name "Bacon" mentioned by one of the men at the bar, and he strained to catch the conversation.

". . . stay in town," a cowboy was saying to his companion.

"I seen her, Buck," the other man replied, "and she's a real looker."

"She gonna work in town, Danny?"

The cowboy shrugged. "Don' know, but I sure wish the Bitter Creek would hire itself another soiled dove. How 'bout that, Jason?" he asked the bartender.

Jason merely smiled and continued wiping his ever-present glass.

Jeremiah walked up behind the two cowboys and tapped Danny on the shoulder. "Excuse me," he said.

"Huh?" the man grunted and, still holding a mug of beer in his right hand, slowly pivoted on his elbow until he was sideways to Jeremiah. Jason stopped wiping his glass, and the other cowboy looked up into the mirror to see Jeremiah's reflection.

"What's a soiled dove?" Jeremiah asked.

The man guffawed and stared at Jeremiah, examining his clothes. The other cowboy tried to stifle a laugh by burying his chin in his chest, and the bartender chuckled and started wiping his glass again.

"A soiled dove," Danny explained, hooking the thumb of his left hand in his gunbelt and grinning, "is a whore, a tart, a—a—"

"A prostitute?" Jeremiah suggested.

"Fancy word for it, but, yeah, that's what—"

Jeremiah swung at the man's head with his fist. The cowboy's head snapped back, partly from the glancing blow but mostly as an avoidance maneuver. The beer in the mug splashed up and soaked the bartender's apron.

"Hey!" Jason yelled.

Danny didn't hesitate, but dropped the mug and landed a well-aimed punch on Jeremiah's jaw. Jeremiah stumbled backward, his head reeling, and he tumbled over a chair, knocking it and another down, all three of them landing with a crash and clatter on the floor.

"Fight!" someone hollered.

"Hot damn, a brawl, come on!"

Jeremiah rolled to his side and got to his hands and knees. He shook his head and then rose unsteadily to his feet. He lunged at Danny, who was now dancing in front of him, his fists shadowboxing. Jeremiah swung violently again. Danny ducked and smashed a fist into Jeremiah's stomach, forcing the air out of him. Jeremiah staggered backward again, his eyes wide, and Danny was after him.

"Hold it!" Otis MacKenzie's voice boomed out. All movement in the saloon stopped instantly, except for Jeremiah, who renewed his attack.

"Call 'im off, Marshal," Danny said, grabbing Jeremiah's wrists and wrestling with him. "I stopped, I quit."

"I can see that," Otis said, reaching the two struggling men. "Knock it off, Bacon," he ordered. Easily the marshal tossed Jeremiah against a table, then took a position between the antagonists.

"Bacon?" Danny asked, startled.

"He insulted my mother, Marshal," Jeremiah accused. "He called her a prostitute!"

Otis whirled his head around and glared at the cowboy. "What?"

Danny took a step back. "It was just talk, Marshal," he said, holding his hands up. "I wouldn't've said it if I'd knowed this Bacon feller was behind me."

"The kid swung first, Marshal," Buck put in. "Didn't even give Danny here a chance to say nothin'."

"S'right, Marshal," Danny agreed quickly. "Hell, I'da said I was sorry if he'da given me half a chance."

"All right," the lawman said, raising his hand to cut off the debate. "It's over, you're even."

"But—" Jeremiah protested.

"Come on," Otis said, grabbing Jeremiah by the arm. "You were both out of line."

"But he—"

"If you think you've been wronged, you gotta give the other fellow a chance to right it before you strike," the marshal explained, dragging the reluctant young man toward the other end of the bar.

They stopped in front of a moderate-sized man in a gray suit, with a large gold chain hanging out of the pocket of a bright red vest. The man's slightly balding head was counterbalanced by a bushy mustache. He held a cigar in his left hand.

"Mel," Otis said to the man, "this is Jeremiah Bacon." He waved a hand toward the saloon owner. "Mel Zwieg, your new employer."

"Otis," Zwieg said, squinting at the marshal. "You didn't tell me he was a hothead to boot."

"I'll keep him in line," Otis declared. "Don't worry."

"Hmph. Well, pleased to meet you, Jeremiah," Zwieg said, extending a hand.

Jeremiah doubted his sincerity but shook his hand politely anyway. "Pleasure," he said formally. Then he rubbed his throbbing jaw.

"Don't misjudge the cowboy," Zwieg said. "He really has the deepest respect for your mother, for any virtuous woman."

"A good woman's the eternal dream of a cowhand, Bacon," Otis explained. "Can't get a wife while he's workin'—no money, no time, no place to keep one. He wouldn't've said what he did if he'd known you were there. And he probably wouldn't've said it at all if he'd heard your mother singin' at the grave. Jees, I thought her singin' would yank the nails right out of the coffin lid."

Jeremiah quieted down. Perhaps he'd been hasty; the man seemed genuinely apologetic when he had heard Jeremiah's identity. He realized he probably didn't understand the people here. This wasn't Boston; it was their country.

"Marshal here says you can play piano," Zwieg said.

"Yes, sir," Jeremiah replied.

"I can use a piano player. Keeps the customers happy and buyin'. Girls need someone to play for their show."

"How much does it pay?" Jeremiah asked.

"I'll start you at a dollar a night Friday and Saturday to see how you do. A free meal gets thrown in,"

Zwieg emphasized, motioning to the end of the bar where there was a spread of eggs, bread, slices of meat, biscuits, beans, and some cheese. "No pay the other nights, but you can eat here and keep any tips and drinks from the customers if you want to come in and play. Week-nights are slow around here."

Jeremiah nodded. "When can I start?"

Zwieg waved a hand toward the piano. "Right now. Come on, I'll show you the piano."

"Mel," Otis interrupted, "I'll leave you with Bacon. Goin' back to the office."

"Right, Otis," Zwieg said, "see ya."

Zwieg led Jeremiah to the piano. It was a wreck. There were gouges and scratches everywhere, and innumerable rings, where an equal number of wet beer mugs had rested, intermingled in a confused network. Cigar burns were on the arms, some of the keys had lost their ivory, and two keys on the very bottom of the keyboard were actually missing. A large, jagged hole was ripped in the wood, about chest-high if a man was sitting down. Jeremiah pointed to it.

"Bullet hole," Zwieg informed him. "That's how we lost our last piano player, Freddy."

"Someone shot him?" Jeremiah asked, frightened.

"Yeah," the man said. Then he chuckled, noting Jeremiah's expression. "Oh, it wasn't for the way he played. Two cowhands at the table behind him got into a pistol fight over some card cheatin', bullet went wild, and . . ." Zwieg gestured toward the hole.

Jeremiah swallowed. He pulled the swivel piano stool out and sat down, pulling himself a little closer. His hands descended slowly to the keyboard and struck a chord. He winced. The piano was woefully out of tune, and the dissonance grated on his ears.

"Nice, huh?" Zwieg commented, smiling.

Jeremiah looked at him appalled, but said nothing.

"Well," the saloon owner said, slapping Jeremiah on the shoulder, "go to it."

Jeremiah nodded as Zwieg turned and strode back to his office, leaving the door open. He sighed as he perused the keyboard. Trying a few more chords did nothing to change his first impression of the piano. Terrible. And middle C didn't play at all; the bullet that had killed his predecessor had also killed middle C.

What to play? Jeremiah decided to start with an excerpt from the first movement of Tschaikowsky's concerto for piano in B flat minor, which had its world premiere in Boston not five years previously and was widely popular there. He began playing, pained by what the abused piano did to the Russian's beautiful music.

"Hey," Zwieg interrupted, not two minutes into the selection. Jeremiah stopped playing and looked up. "You tryin' to put my customers to sleep or somethin'?" the man asked sarcastically.

"This is a highly acclaimed concerto, Mr. Zwieg," Jeremiah protested. "One of Tschaikowsky's finest works for—"

"Don't you have somethin' livelier? This isn't a wake."

"Well, I—uh—"

"Somethin' like 'Golden Slippers'? A new song just out last year. Or maybe 'Buffalo Gals'?" Zwieg looked at Jeremiah hopefully.

"No," Jeremiah said, chagrined at not being able to oblige his employer but also a little insulted to have someone think he should be interested in anything as pedestrian as minstrel-show tunes.

"Well—" Zwieg shifted the cigar in his mouth. "Hey, Jason," he called to the bartender. "Didn't Freddy leave some music around?"

"Yeah," Jason answered. "It's in the back room. Want me to get it?"

"Right—and hurry," Zwieg urged. "This boy needs help."

Jason returned quickly with a small stack of sheet music, which he handed to Jeremiah.

"There you go," Zwieg said. He tapped a finger on the pile. "Find some stuff in there and play that." Then he returned to his office, again leaving the door open.

Jeremiah sighed in resignation and began paging through the music: "Camptown Races," "Turkey in the Straw," "Oh, Them Golden Slippers," "Bury Me Not on the Lone Prairie," "Buffalo Gals," and others. Most of the sheets were commercially sold sheet music, but the rest were scores sloppily penciled in on musically lined paper.

"Golden Slippers" had been one of the songs mentioned by Zwieg, and Jeremiah decided to start with that one. He set the open sheet music against the face of the piano and began to play. A lively tune; Jeremiah begrudgingly admitted to himself that perhaps it was more appropriate to the occasion and crowd.

He was startled to hear several men break into voice as he was playing the chorus. And when he finished, there was a shout of "Play it again!" So he did. The chorus was louder than the first time. When he finished, a couple of men clapped.

"You're a lot better than the other piano plunker, mister," someone commented. A chair scraped, and a man walked up to the piano.

"You know 'Sweet Betsy From Pike'?" he asked.

Jeremiah riffled through the papers, remembering having seen that title. He put up the music and played the lead-in.

"Hold it a minute," someone from behind him said. "I'll join you, Sandy."

"Me, too."

Jeremiah waited until the other men came up to the piano, mugs in hand. Then he began to play.

"Oh, don't you remember Sweet Betsy from Pike,
  Who crossed the big mountains with her lover Ike."

Jeremiah was unexpectedly impressed. It had not
occurred to him that men in a place like this would
have an appreciation for any kind of music, but it was
obvious that these men were familiar with the music
and enjoyed singing. They knew all the words, and
their voices were not unpleasant, blending well together. Emotions released by alcohol, they sang lustily,
even if off key sometimes, and ignored the piano often.

"Hey, keypuncher, what's your name?" one fellow
asked.

"Jeremiah Bacon."

"Well, that's an uncommon handle. Won't forget
that one. Pound those keys."

Other men joined the group, adding their voices
and enthusiasm. keeping time to the music by swinging their beer mugs back and forth.

"The Shanghai ran off and their cattle all died,
  That morning the last of the bacon was fried,
  Poor Ike was—"

The singing fell apart as a general fit of laughter
commenced.

"They ate the piano player!"

"Cannibals!"

Jeremiah stopped playing and stared patiently at
the music. His name had made him the butt of jokes
since his school days had begun; it would probably
be a life-long affliction.

The singing resumed, and the men sang verse after
verse. They had verses that weren't even on the sheet
music, and, with much bickering, they even went
back and repeated previous verses.

"Saying goodby, dear Isaac, farewell for a while,
  But come back in time to replenish my pile."

The conclusion brought a general round of laughing and clapping in self-approbation.

"Now 'Old Paint,'" someone suggested.

"No, first a drink for the piano player," another demanded.

"No, thanks," Jeremiah spoke up, but he was ignored. There was extensive agreement with the original suggestion, and the man who had made it hailed Jason. The bartender quickly brought a mug of beer on a tray, and the cowboy swept it off the tray and tossed a dime onto the latter.

"Here you go, Bacon," the man offered.

Jeremiah looked at the grinning cowboy, a man with a rugged face with a noticeably flattened nose. He wore a black vest over a black-and-white plaid shirt, and a tan hat was pushed back on his head. Jeremiah raised his hand to push away the mug.

"No, thanks," he repeated. "I don't drink alcoholic beverages."

"What? Don't drink?"

"That's unnatural," someone added with concern.

"'Bout time you learned then, piano player," the cowboy with the mug insisted. He thrust it under Jeremiah's nose, and Jeremiah pushed it away, splashing some of the contents onto the piano keys.

"Drink it, don't spill it," the man scolded. He brought the mug up to Jeremiah's mouth and tried to force it between his lips.

"Pour it in 'im, Gordie," a man urged.

"Cut it out," Jeremiah snapped. He rose to his feet. "Don't push me."

Gordie feigned shock at Jeremiah's bold resistance. "Help me, boys," he said. "We gotta learn this feller somethin'."

Enthusiastically the crowd pounced upon Jeremiah, sweeping him off his feet and holding him horizontally. With two men holding his head, the mug of beer was poured over Jeremiah's face. Some of the brew actually went into his mouth, but more of it went up his nostrils, and most of it splashed onto the floor.

Jeremiah coughed and jerked his head about violently. He thrashed about, struggling to break the vise-like grip of the men, who were all laughing uproariously.

"This Bacon feller's a regular fire-breathin', back-breakin', foot-stompin' mustang," Gordie declared. "What say we cool him off in the trough outside?"

"Yeah! Right! Into the trough!"

The men lurched toward the front door, Jeremiah struggling and protesting the entire way. He caught sight of Zwieg standing at the bar.

"Mr. Zwieg! Mr. Zwieg!" he pleaded.

Zwieg waved and smiled.

With difficulty, the men managed to get Jeremiah through the front door and carry him over to the trough. Swinging him in an arc, the group loudly counted to three. The young man flew through the air, flailing helplessly with all four limbs. He landed in the trough with a huge splash that soaked several of the men in front, and he banged his head on the side of the trough.

Laughing and slapping each other on the back, the men returned to the saloon. Jeremiah struggled to his feet and stood in the trough, panting and fuming with rage, as the water gushed off his clothes. A grinning Zwieg, one hand in his pocket and the other rotating the cigar in his mouth, stood on the boardwalk, next to the saloon girl in the red dress, who was chuckling to herself.

"Mr. Zwieg!" Jeremiah addressed the man. "Is this the way you let your employees be treated?"

"Whatever keeps the customers happy," the man replied.

"Well, I'll be damned if—" Jeremiah stopped. That was the first time he'd ever used the word "damn" in an exclamation, but it felt good. "I'll be damned," he repeated, "if I'm going to tolerate such behavior."

Zwieg took the cigar out of his mouth and stepped off the boardwalk. With a stern visage he wagged the end of the cigar at Jeremiah. "Now listen, Bacon," he reprimanded. "I didn't want to hire on a greenhorn, snotnose, spoiled kid from Boston, but since the marshal says I have to, you'll at least work the way I want you to. Your job is to keep the customers happy, and if keepin' 'em happy means you get dumped in that horse trough, then, by God, you get dumped in the horse trough! Understand?"

Jeremiah wiped the water from his face with a hand, trying to control his anger. "Yes, sir," he said. If only he didn't need the job so badly.

"Good," Zwieg said. "Now go back in there, get a beer, and drink it. To refuse an offer of a drink from a man is to tell him you think you're better than he is. So, take the beer, nurse it all night. Any others you get just let pile up on the piano. Jason'll come along later and pour 'em back in the keg."

"Yes, sir," Jeremiah repeated.

Zwieg stuck the cigar back in his mouth. He glanced at Jeremiah's temple. "Looks like you got cut," he said, his tone softening. "Stacey," he said, turning to the saloon girl, "take him around back and get him patched up. See if you can find some of Freddy's old clothes for him, too."

"What?" the girl protested. "Since when am I a nursemaid that has to wipe a man's nose when—"

Zwieg glowered at her.

"Okay, okay," she acquiesced. She turned on her heels and headed for the corner of the saloon. "This way, Bacon," she said curtly. Zwieg headed for the front door.

Jeremiah sloshed his way out of the water trough and felt the bump and cut on his head. Dripping profusely, he followed Stacey around to the back of the building. They came in through the back door into the hallway and then entered a door there that opened into a large room. The room was stacked with

supplies, mostly cases and kegs of liquor and beer.
Jason was in the room. He had four empty liquor
bottles standing in a row on a box, and he was filling
each one a third full of water from a pitcher.

"Sit," Stacey ordered, pointing to a box. Jeremiah
complied. She picked up a rag and started dabbing
at the cut on his head. From six inches Jeremiah
took his first real look at the saloon girl. She was
slim, with an almost thin face, a long pointed nose
and small pursed lips, heavily laden with lipstick.
Her red-brown hair fell in straggly tresses down onto
her shoulders. Jeremiah's gaze shifted from her brown
eyes down to her lowcut dress, where he had a close
view of a rather large portion of her breasts rising
and falling as she breathed. A powerful, sweet aroma
of perfume assaulted his nose.

"Hold that," she snapped brusquely. Jeremiah
quickly put his hand up to the rag and held it in
place.

Jason opened a bottle of dark liquor, took a long
swig, then gave a sigh of contentment. He offered
the bottle to Stacey.

"Thanks," she said. She put the bottle to her lips
and tilted it back. Bubbles rose through the liquid
as she gulped down long draughts of the bottle's
contents. "Damn good," she pronounced, finishing
the drink. She tossed the bottle back to Jason, who
took another drink. Then he proceeded to fill up the
other bottles.

"What are you doing?" Jeremiah asked.

"Makin' money," the bartender answered, opening
another bottle of liquor.

"Ignorant, ain't he?" Stacey said to Jason. She
turned to Jeremiah. "Take off those wet clothes,
Bacon. I'll dig up some of Freddy's stuff." She left the
room.

Jeremiah pried his clinging wet suit coat off. "Isn't
that dishonest?" he asked the bartender.

"Only if you're caught," Jason said.

Jeremiah undid his tie and removed his shirt. "Mr. Zwieg know you're doing that?"

" 'Course," Jason said. He stopped pouring and looked at Jeremiah. "But he'd take it mighty unkindly if you was to mention this to anyone else. Understand?"

Jeremiah was understanding more all the time. "Right," he said. He finished undressing. Jason headed for the door with an armful of bottles.

Stacey walked in as the bartender was leaving, and she closed the door after him. Jeremiah jumped and grabbed his wet clothes and held them in front of himself. He blushed vividly.

"Hellfire, ain't you somethin'!" she commented. "Here," she added, tossing a bundle of clothes on the box next to Jeremiah. "Some of Freddy's stuff."

"Why were his clothes here?" Jeremiah asked, trying to sound nonchalant.

"He lived here," Stacey informed him. "Supposedly in one of the rooms upstairs, but he spent all his time downstairs. He played the piano so he could drink, and he did a lot of both."

She came up to Jeremiah and reached for the clothes he held. "Gimme those wet things, and I'll hang 'em over the crates to dry." Jeremiah resisted, unwilling to expose himself. "Hellfire, Bacon," she swore. "Don't be such an ass. You think you're the first man I've seen with his pants off?" She tore the clothes from his grasp. "Damnation," she said disgustedly.

Jeremiah leaped for the bundle of clothes she'd brought and quickly placed them strategically in front of himself. Stacey draped the wet clothes over some boxes, and then, without a look back, left the room, slamming the door behind her.

Jeremiah quickly put on Freddy's clothes, which turned out to be rather small. After that he left the room and walked back to the saloon proper, stepping up to the bar with deliberation. He glared at Gordie sitting at one of the tables. The look was returned, and the cowboy mumbled something to the men at the table, at which everybody broke into smiles.

"A beer, Jason," Jeremiah ordered.

"Sure," the bartender said. He filled a mug with beer, scraped off the head level with the top of the mug, and then set it on the bar in front of Jeremiah. "We'll take it outa your pay."

Jeremiah nodded and took the mug by the handle. He walked toward the table where Gordie sat.

"Want us to help you with that one, too?" Gordie asked. The others laughed.

Jeremiah said nothing, but stopped about ten feet away from the table. He raised the mug to his lips and then closed his eyes to concentrate on drinking the foreign-tasting liquid, sour and foamy, and not particularly cool. He didn't take a breath until he had downed the entire contents of the mug. Several of the men applauded, and even Gordie looked impressed.

"That wasn't so hard, was it?" Gordie asked, a smirk on his face.

Incensed, Jeremiah impulsively hurled the mug underhanded at Gordie, who caught it as it hit him on the chest, splashing some residual liquid over his shirt. The cowboy's eyes flashed. He threw the mug to the floor and sprang to his feet. His hand went for the gun strapped to his hip, and the weapon was halfway out of its holster, the hammer cocked, when someone yelled, "He ain't armed, Gordie!" Gordie froze.

Jeremiah was stunned by the man's action. His mouth dropped open, his hands suddenly went moist, and his body tensed. The saloon was ghostly quiet.

Suddenly, a deep belch, the result of having swallowed nearly a pint of frothy beer and a good deal of air coincidentally, issued from Jeremiah's mouth and echoed loudly through the still room.

"Gawd damn," someone exclaimed, "facing a six-gun with a burp."

"Fastest belch west of the Mississippi."

Gordie's anger collapsed under the onslaught of the raucous laughter that rocked the saloon, and he quickly fell in with the joke. "I'm hit!" he cried and staggered backward. He threw himself on the floor. "Help! Help!"

"Quick, somebody, a beer to revive him."

An occupant at the table poured the contents of his mug down onto Gordie's face, the stream wandering from his mouth to his nose and eyes and back again. Gordie lay with his mouth open collecting the deluge of beer until the mug was empty.

"Jason, another beer for the wounded man!"

"No, let's take the wounded to the bar."

With delight and gales of laughter, the spectators grabbed Gordie by his arms and legs and hauled him to the bar. The crowd brushed past Jeremiah as if he weren't there, and he watched as the cowboy was lowered ungently to the floor and cascades of beer washed over his smiling face.

Jeremiah rubbed his own face with his hands, and he noticed how much they were trembling. He realized how close he'd just come to being shot. And he was amazed at the volatility of the man's mood. One second on the verge of murder, the next in a boisterous joke.

Jeremiah returned to the piano and sat down, suddenly very weary. He selected a tune and started playing, and the crowd at the bar moved almost en masse to gather around him, anxious for more singing.

"Oh, Buffalo gals won't you come out tonight,
    Come out tonight, come out tonight."

At the conclusion of each verse the men hooted and clapped and good-naturedly slapped Jeremiah on the back. Someone brought a beer for him, and he immediately took a swallow, then set the mug down on top of the piano. No one took special note of his actions; the recent confrontation apparently had already been forgotten.

The singing went on interminably. Verse after verse, song after song, again and again. By the time the group of singers dispersed, either unable or unwilling to both stand and carry a tune at the same time, it was well past two o'clock. The piano was festooned with mugs full of beer, and a few even sat on the floor. Jeremiah was still nursing the one he'd started on. A few tips had also been left, and, much to Jeremiah's surprise, Gordie had come up just before he left for the night, put his arm around Jeremiah's shoulder, told him from two inches in front of his face that Jeremiah was the "best damn p'ano player nor' or sou' o' Bi'er Creek," and then stuffed a twenty-dollar bill into Jeremiah's shirt pocket.

Zwieg was pleased with Jeremiah's effect on business, and he immediately raised the pay to two dollars a night.

Jeremiah was bushed. His hands ached from the long hours of playing. He retrieved his damp clothes from the back room of the saloon and then headed for the marshal's office. Otis showed him a cell cot he could use, and Jeremiah lay down, still in his clothes, and instantly fell asleep.

CHAPTER FIVE

Saturday, June 18, 1880

Jeremiah opened his eyes slowly and stared at the sunlight coming in through the bars of the cell window. With effort he swung his legs off the cot and onto the floor. He ran his hands over his face and rubbed his eyes, then stretched, rose, and walked sleepily to the office.

"Mornin', Bacon," Otis greeted, turning in his swivel chair. "What's left of it."

"Morning, Marshal," Jeremiah returned. He walked over to a bench along the wall that faced the marshal's desk and slumped down.

"Hear you had yourself quite a time at the Bitter Creek last night," Otis started.

Jeremiah looked at the man somewhat apprehensively.

"Hear you play the piano real good," Otis continued, leaning back in his chair.

Jeremiah nodded, not one to deny his talent.

"Hear you became a beer drinker last night, too," the marshal said with a grin.

Jeremiah just stared at him, wondering what the man was leading up to.

"Also hear," Otis said seriously, leaning forward to fold his hands on the desk, "you almost got yourself killed in a fracas with a cowhand from the Circle G, a fellow by the name of Gordie Hodson."

"Yes, sir," Jeremiah admitted and shuddered again at the recollection.

"You got a chip on your shoulder, Bacon," Otis

said. "In view of the reason for your bein' in Point of Rocks, I can understand why you're not feelin' real friendly. But if you aim to stay here, you're gonna have to learn to fit in better, understand the people."

"I lost my head last night, Marshal," Jeremiah confessed. "I—I don't remember having a temper before my father . . ."

"I understand," the marshal said sympathetically. "Just try to control yourself. Don't cause your mother any more grief."

Jeremiah nodded emphatically. That was the last thing he wanted to do.

The street door opened, and the marshal's deputy stepped in.

"Paul," Otis said in greeting.

"Morning, Otis," the deputy replied, closing the door and taking a look at Jeremiah.

"Paul, this is Jeremiah Bacon," Otis said. "Paul Warner, my deputy."

Jeremiah rose and shook hands with the man. "Pleased to meet you," he said.

"Hello, Jer," Paul said pleasantly. "Sorry about your pa."

"Thanks."

Paul pulled a chair away from the wall and set it down by the side of the marshal's desk. He sat down and propped his feet on the desk, leaning back in the chair.

"Need a shave?" Otis asked, noting the way Jeremiah ran his hand over his chin.

"Yes," Jeremiah answered. "Mind if I use that?" he asked, pointing to a pitcher and basin that sat on a small table in front of a mirror on the wall.

"Go ahead," Otis said. "And after that go over to the Red Desert Mercantile and get yourself a set of duds like these. You'll need some rough clothes if you aim to get any work here besides piano playing."

" can't afford any," Jeremiah said. He had something else in mind for the money he'd gotten the previous night.

"I put some money down on account for you," Otis informed him. "Pay me back when you can."

"Thanks, Marshal," Jeremiah said gratefully. "I'll get my shaving paraphernalia." He returned to the cell.

"Pretty generous with the dude, aren't you, Marshal?" Paul commented.

"Just tryin' to help out," Otis explained.

"Couldn't be you're tryin' to get in good with his ma, could it?" Paul suggested further, a big grin spreading across his face.

Otis gave the deputy's chair a swift kick, knocking it out from under him.

" 'S not funny," Otis snapped.

"Okay, okay," Paul apologized, picking himself off the floor. "I'm sorry."

Jeremiah stepped from the door of the Red Desert Mercantile store. He wiggled his toes inside the ready made boots and tugged at the lapels of the brown leather vest. Resettling the new wide-brimmed hat on his head, he strode briskly to the gunsmith's shop across the street. A small bell tinkled overhead to announce his entrance into the cluttered shop. A distinct odor of machine oil permeated the room.

A small, wiry man with a shock of almost white hair stepped through a curtain from a back room into the store proper and peered at Jeremiah over the top of rimless glasses. "May I help you?" the man asked.

"Mr. Schmidt?" Jeremiah asked in turn.

"Indeed, sir," the man answered, bowing slightly. "Seller and supplier of fine guns and ammunition, gun doctor, watchmaker—"

"I'd like to buy a gun," Jeremiah interrupted.

The man swept his open hand around the store. "Well, you've come to the right place, sir. I have the finest selection of arms between Cheyenne and Salt Lake," Schmidt boasted. "What manner of firearm did you desire?"

"A handgun."

"Revolver, pepperbox, derringer? Single-action or double?"

Jeremiah blinked at the man, bewildered. "Well," he said hesitantly. "Like the marshal's."

"Ah," the gunsmith said, gazing down through the glass top of the counter over which the two men faced each other. "Then you'll probably be interested in a Colt." He reached through the back of the cabinet and brought out a pistol, laying it almost reverentially on the counter in front of Jeremiah. "This," he said profoundly, "is the Colt forty-five, single-action, six-shot revolver, employing center-fire cartridges. Colt calls it 'the Peacemaker.' Macabre sense of humor, don't you think?"

Jeremiah carefully studied the gun, the first he'd seen up close. It was dark, solid, rugged, powerful looking. It had a seemingly intrinsic perfect proportion and conveyed an immediate aura of authority.

"Pick it up," the gunsmith suggested, surmising that Jeremiah was a novice.

Jeremiah complied. He hefted the gun and pointed it at the wall.

"Heavy, isn't it?" Schmidt said. "Two pounds five ounces. Seven-and-a-half-inch barrel. Note the superb balance."

"Yes," Jeremiah agreed eagerly, though he didn't know the difference between a good balance and a bad one.

"The Declaration of Independence of the United States says that God created all men equal," the gunsmith said. He shook his head. "Not true. God merely created all men; Colonel Colt made them equal."

"Oh," Jeremiah said. "Uh—what does single-action mean?"

"You have to cock the gun every time you want to

shoot. Here," he said, taking the pistol from Jeremiah. He cocked the hammer back with his thumb and pulled the trigger, then repeated the operation several times.

"Seems like a lot of work," Jeremiah commented.

"Oh, there are double-action models that cock the hammer for you as you pull the trigger," Schmidt explained, putting the gun down on the counter, "but they're not too popular. The action's heavy, and you have to squeeze so hard that the gun jiggles."

"Mm, well, I—uh—"

" 'Course," the storekeeper said, "Colt's not the only manufacturer." He reached into the case again for another pistol, a black cumbersome-appearing weapon. "This is the Smith and Wesson Schofield forty-five. It's got a unique loading system; the gun 'breaks' like this." He grasped the gun in both hands and the barrel and cylinder assembly pivoted at the front of the frame, exposing the chambers. "See? Now, the Colt," he said, setting the gun down, "loads from the side through a loading gate." He picked up the Peacemaker and flipped a small metal gate at the rear of the cylinder, then turned the pistol butt-end first toward Jeremiah. "You get at one chamber at a time."

"I see," Jeremiah said. He glanced from one pistol to the other, undecided as to even the criteria for choosing between them.

Schmidt tapped his chin with a finger. "There's also the Remington forty-four." He reached to one of the shelves behind him and retrieved a pistol that resembled the Colt but had a triangular piece of metal that extended from the frame up toward the front of the barrel. He handed the gun to Jeremiah.

"Most people say it hasn't the balance of a Colt," the man said critically.

"Yes," Jeremiah said, laying the gun down.

"Say," Schmidt said. "You might be interested in the Frontier Colt. It's just like the Peacemaker, but it's chambered for forty-four cartridges. Takes the same ammunition as the Winchester carbines and rifles." He turned and reached high on the wall, pulling a rifle down. He displayed it lovingly in both hands for Jeremiah.

"A pistol's not worth a damn past forty yards," the gunsmith said. "But a Winchester, like this Seventy-three model, is accurate to two hundred yards. Fifteen shots. You're not properly armed unless you've got both a pistol and a Winchester."

Jeremiah shook his head. "I don't have that much money," he said. "But I guess I'll take the forty-four. Maybe later I can get the Winchester."

"Very well. The Colt is seventeen dollars."

"Okay. How about a holster?"

"Four."

"Okay, a holster, too."

"Fine," Schmidt said, starting to replace his merchandise. "That'll be twenty-one dollars."

Jeremiah laid his precious twenty-dollar bill on the counter and added some coins. Schmidt took a belt and holster out of a box and spread it out on the counter, inserting the forty-four Colt. "Satisfactory?" he asked, quickly scooping up the cash.

"Yes," Jeremiah nodded, gathering in his purchase. He wrapped the belt around the holster to make a compact package, then headed for the door.

"Oh, young man," Schmidt called after him.

"Yes?"

"Perhaps you'd like to consider the purchase of some cartridges for that pistol."

"Oh," Jeremiah said sheepishly. He started back toward the counter. "How much?"

"Two-fifty per hundred."

"I'll take a hundred."

"Fine."

Jeremiah walked into the marshal's office, his bundle still under his arm. Otis was sitting at the desk, an empty glass in front of him, and in the process of removing the cork from a bottle. Paul Warner was sitting on the chair next to the desk, his feet propped up as usual.

"Clothes look better, Bacon," Otis said, glancing up. He started pouring.

"Thanks," Jeremiah said. He nodded a greeting to Paul, who returned it. He set the box of cartridges down and drew the pistol out of its holster, pointing it at Otis. The marshal flinched and stopped pouring, his eyes fixed on the barrel of the forty-four. Jeremiah heard Paul slip his own pistol out of its holster.

"Wait!" Otis snapped, raising three fingers of the hand that held the bottle, stopping Paul from doing something rash.

"Teach me to use this thing," Jeremiah said to the marshal.

Otis let out an explosive sigh and slammed the bottle down.

"Jesus," Paul said and uncocked his pistol.

"The first thing you learn," Otis said angrily, leaping from his chair, "is never to point a gun at a man you aren't prepared to shoot." He ripped the gun from Jeremiah's hand.

"It's not loaded," Jeremiah countered, peeved at the marshal's action.

"The second thing you learn," Otis added, "is that a gun is always loaded. That way nobody'll get shot by an 'empty' pistol." He examined the pistol, twirling the cylinder. Then he tossed it back at Jeremiah, forcefully.

Jeremiah winced as the gun struck him in the stomach.

Otis sat down again. "Where'd you get it? Schmidt's?"

Jeremiah nodded, massaging his stomach.

"I thought you were broke. What'd you use for money?" Otis asked.

"Gordie Hodson tipped me twenty dollars when he left last night."

"Twenty dollars!" Otis repeated, startled. "Hodson tipped you twenty dollars?"

"At the *end* of the night?" Paul put in.

"What'd I do? Break a law or something?" Jeremiah asked sarcastically.

"No. It's just that a cowhand makes about thirty dollars a month. That fellow tipped you about three weeks' wages. That's pretty odd in itself, but I also wonder where he got that much money in the middle of the month. Local cowhands get paid on the first."

Jeremiah saw the implication. "You think Hodson was in on the murder of my father?"

"Could be."

"Well, let's go get him," Jeremiah said impatiently.

"Whoa, not so fast," Otis warned. "He may simply have been drunk enough to tip you a stake he'd been savin' for some time. It doesn't make him a killer. But I'll have a talk with him later."

"I'll go with you," Jeremiah volunteered.

"No," Otis said firmly. "I'll let you know what I find out."

"How about the gun?" Jeremiah asked.

"Bacon," Otis counseled. "The outlaws in the Red Desert Gang have lived with guns for a long time. You'd be a fool to take 'em on, and I want no part of givin' you the idea that a couple o' lessons makes you good enough to go after anyone with a gun."

"You teach me or I'll learn on my own, Marshal," Jeremiah said. "I'm determined."

Otis thought of Priscilla Bacon. She had just lost a husband, and now she was probably about to lose the rest of her family. Somehow he couldn't bear the thought.

"All right," Otis said, relenting. "If you do meet the buzzards, I'd rather have them get killed than you." He rose from his chair. "How about some target practice, Paul?"

"Sure," the deputy agreed, adjusting the holster at his side.

The marshal led the other two men to the eastern edge of the town, where they were many rock outcroppings, much lower than the eleven-hundred-foot gray sandstone cliffs north and south of Point of Rocks. Against the small outcroppings corrals had been built, saving the labor of constructing at least one fence side. The rocks formed a natural backstop for use as a firing range, and the wood fence rails were used by any onlookers.

En route to the area the marshal had made a special effort to collect an entourage of the town's boys and barflies, and he made no move to start the proceedings until the rails were well populated and a crowd of boys mingled among the three shooters.

"Why the wait?" Jeremiah asked, puzzled.

"I like to get a crowd before I start throwin' lead," Otis explained. "A lawman works best if the men he runs up against respect him, and in these parts respect is ninety-five percent fear. They," he emphasized, nodding toward the observers, "are the best means I have of makin' sure that it's well-known how good I am. And they'll make me out to twice as good as I really am."

Jeremiah nodded at the man's logic.

"Match you six cans," Otis suggested to his deputy.

"You're on," Paul said.

"Kevin," Otis called to one of the older boys, "set up a dozen cans." The boy jumped to obey, herding several smaller boys, who scrounged up a dozen cans and set them on small rocks that lay on the ground in front of the outcropping. Kevin kept another can for himself, and all the boys scurried for the fence.

The marshal and his deputy stood side by side facing the cans, their hands poised over the handles of their six-guns.

"Toss it," Otis called to Kevin.

Kevin wound up and threw the can as hard as he

could. It arced high into the air and then landed in the dust with a soft bonk. Jeremiah watched in amazement as the two men rapidly drew and emptied their pistols, pulling the triggers and cocking the hammers so fast that the twelve shots came in one short, continuous crash. He involuntarily threw his hands up to his ears to muffle the roar of the Colts, but put them down again, embarrassed, when he noticed that no one else had done the same.

A huge cloud of white smoke drifted back over the men, and Jeremiah squinted at the sting. Through the haze he saw that all of the marshal's cans had disappeared, knocked off their perches. Two of Paul's cans stood in their original positions in mocking silence.

"Nice shootin', Marshal," one of the audience called. Some boys whistled and clapped, and another handful of them swept around the two gunmen, picking up the empty shells that Otis and Paul ejected onto the ground.

They finished loading their pistols and replaced them in the holsters.

"That—that was amazing!" Jeremiah said, awed.

"Comes with practice," Otis said modestly. "Which is why I've got the edge on virtually any man comin' into town. Their job is ranchin' or minin' or clerkin' or whatever. They don't have the time to stand around practicin'. My job is shootin'. And I'd rather do my shootin' at tin cans than at some drunken cowboy who's gotten his courage out of a bottle." He stepped aside. "Okay, Bacon, let's see what you can do."

Jeremiah strapped on the holster and positioned the gun as he had seen the marshal do. He stepped up to the firing line, his pulse speeding.

"Hey, Bacon," a man on the fence called, "aren't you afraid of gettin' powder on your hands?" Others joined him in laughing.

Jeremiah tried to ignore the heckling. He drew the pistol, raised it to eye-level, cocked the hammer, sighted along the top of the gun at one of the cans that the boys had set up again, and pulled the trigger. Nothing happened.

"Oh," he said, quickly reaching for the box of cartridges. "I forgot to load it."

Otis and Paul gave each other knowing looks, and the deputy shook his head sadly. The spectators on the fence howled in glee.

Jeremiah tore off the paper wrapper and stuffed some cartridges into his vest pocket, then tossed the box down. He held the Colt in his left hand and flipped open the loading gate as he had seen the gunsmith do. After inserting a cartridge, he tried to rotate the cylinder, but it wouldn't move. Otis reached over and wordlessly cocked the hammer halfway. Avoiding the marshal's look, Jeremiah rotated the cylinder and carefully filled each chamber, then closed the loading gate.

Again Jeremiah aimed at one of the cans and pulled the trigger. This time the gun jumped in his hand, and smoke drifted back into his face. The bullet kicked up a small dust cloud about ten feet shy of the target and several feet to the side.

The two lawmen chuckled, and a general hooting went up from the fence.

"You need elevation, Bacon," Otis said. "The bullet's droppin' all the time it's in the air. The farther away the target, the more the bullet drops, and the higher above the target you have to aim. Try again."

Jeremiah aimed the pistol again, cocked the hammer, and fired. The bullet dug a hole in the sandstone outcropping behind the targets.

"Overcorrection, Bacon," Otis coached. "Another thing, every gun is a little different. The barrel can't be absolutely aligned with the chamber. So it might shoot a little to the left, maybe a little to the right, a little high, a little low. You'll notice it after a while and have to correct for it. Okay. Shoot."

Jeremiah fired four more times, and each time the

bullet either dug into the dirt or smacked into the rocks. More laughter.

To eject the empty cartridges, he followed the marshal's example. He held the gun in his right hand, flipped open the loading gate, and tilted the gun back. With his left hand he pulled down on a tab located at the far end of a second tube that ran along the bottom of the barrel. The spent shell casing dropped to the ground. He half-cocked the hammer, and then, rotating the cylinder and working the ejector, he clumsily emptied the gun.

Jeremiah then reloaded the pistol and again went through the procedure of cocking, aiming, and firing. His fourth bullet tore into one of the cans and sent it sailing to bounce noisily off the rocks behind it and clunk onto the dirt. Jeremiah's eyes widened, and a smile burst across his face. "I hit it!" he cried and turned to face the marshal, still holding the pistol waist-high.

Paul jumped to the side, and Otis smacked the pistol away with his hand. "Don't point it at anybody!" he reprimanded.

"Sorry," Jeremiah said meekly, quickly lowering the gun. "I forgot."

"Well, don't forget," Otis said sternly. "All right, next let's take a look at the draw." He stood facing the targets. "When you draw," he instructed, "keep your eye on the target. Reach for the gun; pull on the handle slightly until the hammer clears the holster. Place your thumb on the hammer as you continue to pull the gun out. Cock it as you go. Raise the gun away from the holster while lowerin' your thumb around the handle to get a better grip. Don't raise your gun all the way to your eye level unless you have plenty of time. Extend the gun slightly, aim through coordination of hand and eye. Then shoot." The marshal fired and knocked one of the cans off its rock. "You try it," he said. "Slow at first."

Jeremiah faced the targets and went through the

same motions as the marshal, drawing the pistol out of its holster, cocking, aiming, firing. The shot went high.

"Again," Otis said. "Keep tryin'."

Jeremiah did it again, and again the bullet plowed into the outcropping. He tried yet another time, but the gun gave only an impotent click when he pulled the trigger.

"There's another lesson for you, Bacon," Otis said, having anticipated that the gun wouldn't fire. "Always count your shots. Always know how many live rounds you've got in your gun. And replace the empty cartridges at every opportunity, not just when you've used all six of 'em. You never know when you'll need all of 'em in a big hurry."

Jeremiah nodded, absorbing the lessons. He reloaded the forty-four and went through the draw again, slowly, deliberately. His third shot hit one of the cans. He grinned and looked at the marshal, but he was careful to keep the gun pointing toward the rocks.

Otis nodded approvingly. "Okay, now try it fast."

Jeremiah poised himself facing the cans. He paused, then drew and shot a bullet into the dirt not six inches in front of his own boot.

"Jesus, don't shoot your foot off!" Otis exclaimed. Raucous laughter rose from the fence, and Paul had a grin from ear to ear.

"Better stick to the piano," a man shouted.

"You'll be safer with your hands in your pockets," a boy cried.

"Sorry," Jeremiah said. "I guess I was in too much of a hurry." He glared at the catcalls coming from the fence.

"Don't hurry," Otis cautioned. "Speed is important, but so is accuracy. If it ever comes to a shoot-out face to face you'll only get one shot. Make it count."

Jeremiah nodded. Again he drew quickly and fired. There was no sign of the bullet.

"Hey, Marshal," someone called from the fence, "that one went clear to Cheyenne."

Jeremiah glared once again at the laughing and this time swung his pistol around and pointed it at the men. The laughter ceased immediately, and the fence cleared instantly, spectators falling and throwing themselves on the ground and behind posts.

"God damn it!" Otis cried and seized Jeremiah's gun, violently twisting it out of his hand. "How many times I gotta tell you? Don't point the gun at anybody!"

"I just wanted to scare them into being quiet," Jeremiah said, still glaring at the men, but also holding his sore hand.

Otis grabbed Jeremiah by the front of his shirt and yanked him roughly toward himself. "If it weren't for your mother, Bacon, I'd put you on the next train outa here," he snarled. "You're trouble, I can smell it a mile off. Your father was killed, and I'm sorry about that, and I understand why you want to get the Red Desert Gang, but, God damn you, don't take it out on my town!" Otis shoved the startled young man backward.

Jeremiah gulped at the display of the marshal's wrath. "I—I guess I was wrong, sir," he said.

"Damn right you were," Otis said. "Kevin there, ten years old, shoots better than you do. You're so bad you're funny. They got a right to laugh."

Jeremiah shifted his feet uneasily.

"And another thing, Bacon," Otis went on, "pointing a gun at a man gives him the right to defend himself, to shoot first if he can."

"The gun wasn't cocked," Jeremiah timidly pointed out.

"They didn't know that," Otis countered.

The marshal paced about for a moment, letting his temper cool. "All right, Bacon," he said firmly and handed the gun back to Jeremiah. "I've shown you how. Now all you need is practice. Practice, practice, and more practice. It's gotta become natural and unthinkin'."

"I understand," Jeremiah said.

"I'll leave you here. Keep practicin'. Come here anytime. The kids there'll help in settin' up cans and such. Give 'em a tip once in a while."

"Okay."

"Paul and I are goin' back to town. Saturday's a big day, and I like to show the badge as much as possible. See you later." He motioned to Paul, and the two of them headed for the main street.

Otis turned around. "And, Bacon," he said. "Just so you don't ever get too cocky, remember, tin cans don't shoot back. Another man will."

"I'll remember, sir," Jeremiah said. "And, Marshal—thanks."

"Stay alive, Bacon," Otis returned.

CHAPTER SIX

Jeremiah swung open the doors of the Bitter Creek Saloon at nine o'clock and stepped into bedlam; the place was jammed. The bar was packed, every chair in the room was taken. Men leaned against the wall, others stood about, and four cowboys sat on the stage, playing poker. Stacey and the other saloon girl, Dottie, were both surrounded by clusters of customers. A thick haze obscured Jeremiah's vision, his nose was assaulted by the strong smell of tobacco, beer, and liquor, and a loud buzz of talking, laughing, and singing filled his ears.

Jeremiah walked up to the end of the bar where the food was spread. Zwieg was standing there. "Evening, Mr. Zwieg," Jeremiah said.

"Good evening, Jeremiah," Zwieg said merrily, all smiles.

"Business looks good tonight," Jeremiah commented. He picked up some bread and slices of meat and made a sandwich.

"Good? It's terrific! Some of the ranches south of Bitter Creek just took delivery of a herd of Texas steers. The Texas boys just got a couple o' months' wages and aim to spend most of it here tonight."

Jeremiah nodded as he munched on the sandwich and grabbed a piece of cheese.

"Play good tonight, Jeremiah," Zwieg advised him. "Keep 'em happy and buyin'." He turned and headed for his office.

Jeremiah nodded again, his mouth full of food.

"Oh," Zwieg said, pausing for a moment, "the girls have their show about eleven o'clock. There's music for it, called 'Naughty, Naughty Men.' Probably with that music of Freddy's."

"Okay," Jeremiah said between bites. He finished the sandwich and reached for a hard boiled egg. Then he ate a second egg and another large piece of cheese along with another meat sandwich. The meal was free, and he didn't eat much the rest of the day.

After finishing the food he went to the piano and sat down. A cowboy joined him immediately. "Heard you play pretty good," the man said. "Well, I'm a coyote, and tonight's my night to howl. Play 'Oh, Susanna!' for me."

Jeremiah obliged the eager fellow, and the latter had barely started singing when he was joined by other men, full of liquor and enthusiasm and eager to holler off some steam.

The evening's singing had a particularly cowboy flavor to it, Jeremiah having repeatedly to go through songs like "I Ride an Old Paint," "Streets of Laredo," "Bury Me Not on the Lone Prairie," and "Old Chisholm Trail." It struck him as odd that the songs were often sad and melancholy, not at all consistent with the setting.

"Take me to the graveyard and lay the sod o'er me,
For I'm a poor cowboy and I know I've done wrong."

or

"Oh, bury me not on the lone prairie,
Where the wild coyote will howl o'er me."

It seemed incongruous that the men wanted to sing songs like those, speaking as they did of death, loneliness, sadness, and hardship. And he was having a hard time playing, having just buried his father the day before. Perhaps the songs were a way of thumbing their noses at their hard lot, defiance in the face of adversity. Or maybe it was all a false bravado, a façade, none of the men wishing to admit to another how homesick he really was.

Regardless, Jeremiah was glad when they gave up an hour and a half later, leaving the piano cluttered with beers and a few tips. To undo the damage to his own spirits, he spent the next twenty minutes playing all the cheerful and lively tunes he could find in his stack of sheet music.

After that Jeremiah searched through the sheets for the music for the girls' show, but he found nothing that corresponded to the title Zwieg had mentioned. Neither girl was visible at the moment, so he went up to the bar.

"Jason," he said, getting the bartender's attention. "Where are the girls?"

The bartender looked around the room himself, then shrugged. "Probably upstairs." He returned to talking to the men in front of him.

Jeremiah walked back toward the piano and ascended the stairs. He had no idea which of the several doors was the girls' or even if they had separate rooms. He picked one at random and knocked.

A mumbled reply from Stacey satisfied him, and he opened the door and took a step in. "Stacey," he said, "I need the music for—"

"Who the hell?" a man bellowed from the bed as he rose on an elbow.

"Get the hell outa here, Bacon!" Stacey screamed at him from where she lay next to the man.

"I—I—" Jeremiah stammered, still holding the doorknob, frozen by the sight of the two naked people in bed.

"I paid my five dollars, and, by God, I'm gettin' my money's worth," the man declared. He threw himself across Stacey, reaching for the table at the other side of the bed.

"Ya big ox," Stacey hollered and cuffed him on the side of his head.

The man whirled clumsily, a pistol in his hand, and fired blindly at the doorway. Jeremiah heard the bullet whiz past his head at the instant he heard the explosion of the report, magnified in the confines of the small room. The bullet smacked into the wall on the other side of the hall and sent fragments of wood and plaster flying.

Jeremiah leaped backward around the corner of the doorway.

"Close the damn door!" Stacey ordered.

Jeremiah reached for the doorknob in a lightning move and pulled hard, jumping back. A bullet burst through the door near the top just as it slammed shut. Jeremiah sank to his knees, shaking.

"Watch your stinkin' feet," Stacey snapped. Jeremiah could hear them thrashing about on the bed. Yet another bullet crashed through the wood and buried itself in the hallway wall. "Put the damn iron back on the table, cowboy," Stacey screeched.

Jeremiah scurried on his hands and knees for the stairs. Just as he reached the head, Jason mounted the top, a sawed-off shotgun in his hands. "What's all the shootin' about?" he asked anxiously, his eyes darting about the hallway, noting the little cloud of plaster dust hanging there.

Stacey and the cowboy were still shouting at each other. Jason ran for the door and pounded on it, careful to stand to the side. "Stacey!" he yelled. "You all right?"

"Yeah, I'm all right," she answered. "This cowboy's trigger-happy, is all."

"Well, I—" the customer protested.

"Aw, shut up," she snarled. "I'm okay, Jason. Just tell that jackass piano player he's gotta wait in line like everybody else."

Jeremiah flushed at the mention of himself. He was still on his hands and knees at the head of the stairs, and he suddenly realized that almost everybody in the saloon was staring at him. He backed away and sat up against the wall. Jason came up, dangling the shotgun in one hand, its barrel swinging in front of Jeremiah's face.

"What were you doin'?" the bartender asked, not angrily, just out of curiosity.

"Well, you said they were upstairs," Jeremiah explained, "and I wanted to get that music for the show, so I—"

The bartender laughed. "What'd you think the girls was doin' up here on a Saturday night?" He laughed again. "Don't worry 'bout the music; they'll get it to you before the show."

Jason lifted Jeremiah by one arm, and the two of them went to the stairs and descended. Zwieg, a pistol in his hand, met them at the foot. "Anybody hurt?"

"Just the walls," Jason said. "The piano player got himself an education tonight."

Zwieg's expression turned from worry to amusement. He smiled at Jeremiah and chuckled.

"I didn't mean to . . ." Jeremiah tried to explain.

"Aw, don't worry about it," Zwieg said. "I just get kinda shook when the lead flies upstairs. I got a hard time gettin' girls for this place; hate to see my investment shot to hell." He turned his attention to the crowd. "Okay, everybody, back to the fun."

Otis MacKenzie entered the saloon, a gun in his hand, but he was in the process of reholstering it, apparently having judged the situation as peaceful. He walked up to Jeremiah and Zwieg. "I heard shootin'," he said.

"A gun-happy cowhand, Marshal," Zwieg explained. "He took a couple o' shots at your protégé here, when he broke in on 'em upstairs."

The marshal looked at Jeremiah and nodded. Jeremiah couldn't miss the disapproval in the look.

"How 'bout sittin' in on a game, Otis?" Zwieg asked.

"All right," Otis agreed.

Zwieg led Otis to one of the tables where some of the better-heeled customers were playing poker, and he invited himself and the marshal into the game. Jeremiah went back to the piano.

The cowboy from upstairs came down shortly thereafter and sneered at Jeremiah as he went by. A few minutes later Stacey appeared at the railing of the balcony and contemptuously dropped several sheets of music onto the stage. Jeremiah rushed to pick up the papers and hurried back to the piano. He noted the title of "You Naughty, Naughty Men" from the 1886 hit show, *The Black Crook*. Stacey was joined by Dottie, and she motioned Jeremiah to commence.

Jeremiah started to play. Some of the men immediately recognized the theme song of the girls, and they rushed to crowd around the stage. The girls slowly descended the stairs, all smiles and eroticism, and still wearing the same yellow and red dresses they always wore. The crowd around the stage grew rapidly.

The girls reached the stage to the accompaniment of much cheering and whistling, and they began to cavort about, going through a clumsy routine. Then they started to sing.

> "I will never more deceive you,
> Or of happiness bereave you,
> But I'll die a maid to grieve you,
> Oh, you naughty, naughty men."

Jeremiah had found something that sounded worse than the piano; they were awful. And the dance steps were awkward and ungraceful.

Verse and verse the song went on, and each time the girls reached the part of "naughty, naughty men" they each stood facing the crowd, feet apart, left hand on hip, and wagging a finger at the audience The men roared and cheered.

Jeremiah was grateful when the last verse arrived.

"We've no wish to distress you,
We'd sooner far caress you,
And when kind, we'll say, 'Oh, bless you:
Oh, you naughty, dear delightful men."

The men thundered their applause and swept the two performers off the stage, rushing them to the bar where they were perched on top. Drinks were ordered all around, and dozens offered to Dottie and Stacey. Jeremiah noticed Zwieg standing in the door of his office, twisting the cigar in his mouth with avaricious delight in his eyes.

After that spectacle, the rest of the evening was anticlimactic. What was worse for Jeremiah—the saloon girls got all the tips.

CHAPTER SEVEN

Sunday, June 19, 1880

Otis MacKenzie lay on his cot, his hands folded in back of his head, his eyes focused on a large bug that explored the adobe wall to his left. He turned as he heard Jeremiah come out of the cell area. The young man walked over to the small table with the water supply and put down his shaving kit.

"You got enough to shave *every* day?" Otis asked, in mock surprise.

Jeremiah glared at him in the mirror as he stirred the lather in the cup.

"Jus' pokin', Bacon," Otis said, chuckling. "Don't get riled."

"How come you're not out making rounds or something?" Jeremiah asked, brushing on the foam.

Otis stretched his arms. "Sunday mornings are dead," he explained. "The real troublemakers are drunken into a stupor, and the rest of the towns-people are on their best behavior. It's my day to sleep in."

The marshal rose and crossed the short distance to his desk and sat down. From a lower drawer he withdrew a bottle and a glass. "Drink?" he asked.

Jeremiah shook his head.

Otis poured himself one, then leaned back in his chair and put his feet on the desk, wiggling his big toes through the holes in his socks.

Jeremiah finished shaving and continued dressing. "I take it you're not coming to church," he said. He brushed at the wrinkles in his suit coat; the dunking in the water trough had not been kind to it.

"Me? Naw," Otis responded. "I haven't seen the inside of a church since my ma died when I was a kid."

"Too bad," Jeremiah said. "You sound like you'd have a good singing voice, a nice bass."

Otis laughed, but he was flattered. "Your mother gonna be there?" he asked impulsively. It then struck Otis that he didn't refer to Jeremiah's mother as his "ma.

"Yes," Jeremiah said, straightening his tie one last time. "Reverend Crockett even talked her into singing a solo."

"That right?" the marshal commented, impressed. "Well, she sure has a fine voice. A fine voice," he emphasized, recalling the graveside dirge.

"See you later, Marshal," Jeremiah said, going through the front door.

"Pray for a poor sinner, Bacon," Otis called after him.

"You need it," Jeremiah said, smiling. He headed for the church at a fast pace, because he could hear the faint strains of singing coming through the open doors of the church as the congregation started the first hymn.

Otis swirled the liquor in the glass in his hand and then watched it quickly reach equilibrium again. He drummed his fingers on the side of the glass. Then he put it down and padded over to a self-standing closet in a corner of the office. Opening it, he pulled out a dark-gray suit. He turned it around, holding it by the hanger and brushing off the fine layer of dust that had accumulated along the shoulder ridge. He checked for moth holes. He rubbed his hand over the stubble on his chin, then eyed the bowl of water that Jeremiah had left standing on the table by the mirror. He hung the suit on the top of the door and headed for the table.

* * *

Otis was sure that he was shaking more hands than the minister. It had started with Mrs. Munford, who had taken him under her wing when he had walked tardily and ill-at-ease into the church service. She bubbled all over him, pumping his hand and expressing delight at seeing him at the service. After the service there was Henkleman, and Osborne, and virtually everyone else in the church. He practically had to fight his way to get up as far as the minister.

"Good morning, Marshal," the Reverend Crockett gushed, a smile beaming from ear to ear at the sight of a lost soul saved. "Honored to have you worship with us this morning."

"Uh—yes—uh, the singin' was beautiful," Otis managed to say.

"We really put our hearts into it," the minister said proudly. "And didn't Mrs. Bacon do a magnificent job with 'Rock of Ages'?"

"Indeed, exceptional," Otis agreed readily.

"And the sermon. How did you like the sermon?"

"Oh—interestin'," he said, even though he'd spent the entire time counting the stitches in the hat of the woman in front of him—one hundred and forty-two.

"Will we see you next Sunday?"

"Uh—sure. Next Sunday."

"Splendid!"

Otis hadn't said next Sunday *in church;* a thing like this could be carried too far. He put his hat on and hurried down the church steps.

"Oh, Marshal MacKenzie," a woman's voice called to him.

Otis saw Priscilla Bacon standing off to one side, her hand raised to get his attention. Anita Kessler and Jeremiah were with her. He whipped off his hat and walked up to the trio.

"Mrs. Bacon," he said in greeting. "Miss Kessler, Mr. Bacon," he added with Sunday formality.

"Good morning, Marshal," Priscilla said, a smile on her face.

"I enjoyed your singin' very much, Mrs. Bacon," Otis complimented. "It was the best part of the service."

"You're so kind," Priscilla said graciously. "As you have been since we arrived in Point of Rocks. I wanted to thank you for all you've done. I understand that you were instrumental in my obtaining employment in Mr. Henkleman's store and also as the town teacher for next fall."

"Oh," Otis said, minimizing his part. "I just pointed out some obvious qualifications to some people and . . ." He shifted his hat in his hands by running the brim through his fingers.

"And you got Jeremiah his job."

"Oh—it's not much." He reversed the direction of the hat running through his fingers.

"And provided him with an account at the mercantile."

"Well—just part o' my job."

"Beyond that which is your duty, Marshal," Priscilla declared, "and I am most appreciative."

"Well," Otis said, glancing down at his hat. "Uh— you're welcome, m'am," he said. He looked into her eyes for a moment but quickly looked away. "I gotta be goin' now," he said. "Mrs. Bacon, Miss Kessler, Mr. Bacon."

The three people nodded a good day to the marshal, and he backed off, then turned and headed for his office.

"Mr. Bacon," Anita asked, "will you have dinner with us this noon?"

"I'd be delighted," Jeremiah accepted. "I don't get the best of food on my own nor at the sa—" he looked at his mother, "—loon."

"Good," Anita said. "And come often; it's your mother's home now, too."

"Now, don't be late, Jeremiah," Priscilla said.

"I won't," Jeremiah assured her. "And thank you, Miss Kessler."

"Anita," she suggested.

"Anita," Jeremiah repeated pleasantly.

"More potatoes, Jeremiah?" Anita asked.

"Mm, yes, thank you," the young man replied. "They're delicious." Jeremiah took one of the potatoes and put it on his plate. He mashed it with a fork and then poured thick, rich, brown gravy over it.

"More roast beef, too?" Priscilla asked, always pleased to see her son with a hearty appetite.

Jeremiah took little convincing and forked another piece of the meat onto his plate. "Superb meal," he said to both women.

"And while you're working on that plateful, Jeremiah," Anita began, "I'd like you to consider a business proposition."

Jeremiah looked up at her. "Oh?"

"Well, my father used to do half of the stage driving himself along with Herb Lambrecht. Now with Father—gone, somebody else will have to take his place. Oh, Herb is willing to help out temporarily, but he also ranches and can't do the job full-time. Marshal MacKenzie thought you had the intelligence and skillful hands that would make you just right for the job."

"Driving a stage?" Jeremiah asked, his fork stopped halfway to his mouth. Priscilla looked at Anita, equally surprised.

"Yes," Anita said, smiling.

"I don't know anything about driving a stagecoach."

"Herb would teach you."

"Surely there must be someone else around who is better qualified than I am," Jeremiah said.

"Perhaps," Anita conceded, "but as the marshal pointed out, you and Wells Fargo now have a special connection."

There was a long pause. "His hands," Priscilla said, obviously worried. "Wouldn't his hands be abused?"

"The drivers often wear gloves, Priscilla," Anita countered.

"Driving a stage?" Jeremiah repeated, mulling over the idea. He put down the fork and rubbed his finger-tips together absently. He, too, wondered what hard physical labor would do to his sense of touch.

"We have a feeder line," Anita explained. "It's a three-day trip. The first day takes you north from Point of Rocks to South Pass City. The second day you go up to Atlantic City and Lander and then back to South Pass City. Third day back to Point of Rocks. Stage leaves here on Mondays and Thursdays. You could take the Monday run and Herb the Thursday. That way you'd still be able to keep the job in the saloon and practice the piano."

"Well . . ." he said skeptically.

"While you're learning, you'd be paid eight dollars for each trip. After you take over on your own, it will be twelve dollars."

"Twelve dollars," Jeremiah said eagerly.

"Bed and meals are provided while you're on the job," Anita added.

"Gee, that sounds pretty good, Mother," Jeremiah said, looking at Priscilla. "The piano playing doesn't pay much."

"Are you sure it won't hurt your hands?" she asked.

"I think I can do it," he said, after deliberating. He turned to Anita. "I *will* do it. When do I start?"

"Tomorrow," Anita said. "Stage leaves at eight sharp; be there at quarter of."

"Yes, m'am."

"Oh, and bring your gun."

"Gun!" Priscilla exclaimed, stunned.

Jeremiah froze. He didn't want to look at his mother. Anita darted glances between the other two table occupants. Had she opened Pandora's box?

"Jeremiah," Priscilla asked sternly. "Have you purchased a weapon?"

Jeremiah picked up his napkin and dabbed at his mouth. Then he set it down carefully. "Yes, Mother," he said as he turned to her. "I bought a pistol."

"Why?"

He drew a deep breath. "To avenge Father—if possible."

" 'Vengeance is mine,' saith the Lord," his mother quoted.

"God helps those who help themselves," he countered.

"The law will take care of your father's murderers. Marshal MacKenzie will apprehend the men."

"I'm not so sure of that, Mother."

Priscilla stared at her son. "You know how your father and I felt about guns. And now you own one. And you'll only get hurt or—killed." Her lower lip began to tremble.

"The marshal is teaching me how to use it," Jeremiah said. "I won't get hurt."

"The marshal is *too* kind," Priscilla stated, recalling her earlier show of gratitude. "Jeremiah, I have heard what goes on in that saloon. And your part in some of it. Fighting, guns, drinking, loose women, gambling. And now you defy your mother. I fear I'll not know you in a short time."

"Mother," Jeremiah pleaded. He didn't know what to say. He had to admit that he'd seen more of the rawer side of life in the last four days than he'd seen in all his previous years, and he suddenly realized that he had acquired a strange, probably malevolent fascination in that life. He heard the tick-tock of the floor clock in the parlor, and the chirping of a few birds outside. Time seemed to crawl painfully forward.

"Mother," he tried again. "I will not leave Point of Rocks until my father's murderers are brought to justice. I will drive the stage and work in the saloon in order to earn money—and to keep up practice on the piano. I will continue to improve my skill with a pistol. I will attempt to capture—or kill—my father's murderers." It was a simple but firm statement of his intentions.

Priscilla continued staring at her son. After a moment she turned to look at Anita, hoping for assistance from the woman, but the latter was discreetly arranging her silverware with extreme precision. "I can see, Jeremiah," his mother said finally, "that my words have fallen on deaf ears."

Jeremiah ached at hearing the pain in her voice. Couldn't she understand?

"Well, we are forgetting ourselves," Priscilla said. "This is not the time nor the place to be engaged in a family debate."

Anita looked from Priscilla to Jeremiah and back to Priscilla, anguish in her eyes. "I'm sorry I started this," she apologized.

"Don't be concerned, child," Priscilla reassured her. "It would have come out eventually. And the stage driving could be very good for Jeremiah."

Jeremiah was proud of his mother. She was always concerned about the feelings of others, regardless of her own discomfiture.

"And now, Anita," Priscilla said, smiling—a little. "How about some of that apple pie you made?"

Jeremiah's first and fourth shots hit two cans.

"You're gettin' better, Mr. Bacon," Kevin said.

"Thanks," Jeremiah replied.

"But you ain't no Otis MacKenzie," another boy piped in from the corral fence.

Jeremiah smiled and slipped six more bullets into the cylinder of his Colt, then holstered it. He faced the cans, his hand poised over the gun butt.

"Figured it was you," Paul Warner said, coming up on Jeremiah from behind.

Jeremiah turned. "Oh, hi, Paul. Want to join me?"

"No, thanks, Jer. Don't need it that much," he said cockily.

"Oh," Jeremiah said. He paused, then drew the pistol and fired. Dust jumped away from the wall of the outcropping. He holstered the gun, drew, and fired again. The bullet twanged away from the rock on which a can was sitting.

"Hear you had dinner over at Anita Kessler's place this noon."

"That's right," Jeremiah confirmed. It must be a small town, he thought.

"Anita's a nice girl, isn't she?"

"Very nice," Jeremiah agreed. He drew and fired again. A can went sailing off the rock.

"Nice shot," the deputy complimented.

"Thanks." Jeremiah's next shot caused a spout of dust to erupt in front of a rock.

"I hope you're not gettin' any ideas 'bout courtin' her, Jer," Paul said, studying the targets.

Jeremiah paused and looked at Paul. "My mother's going to be living with her. She was trying to be friendly." He drew and fired. Another miss.

"I see," Paul said. "Uh—you know Anita's almost wearin' my brand."

Jeremiah looked at the man again. "No, I didn't know that. You two engaged?"

"No," Paul conceded, "but my iron's in the fire, and I've almost got her throwed."

"Oh." Jeremiah paused. "But actually, you don't have exclusive claim to her as yet."

"Well, not exactly," Paul said. "But I'd sure take it unkindly for someone to try to cut her out and put his own brand on her."

"I'd say that was up to her to choose," Jeremiah stated. He drew and fired his last shot. It dug a hole in the outcropping.

"I wouldn't say that," Paul said. He drew his own Colt and squeezed off three quick shots and sent each of the remaining three cans whirling away to smack noisily into the outcropping. "No, I wouldn't say that at all." He gave Jeremiah a quick but sinister glance, then turned on his heels and swaggered back toward the main street.

Jeremiah looked first at the deputy, then at the three cans, then back at the deputy. Rapidly he emptied his pistol of the empty cartridges. "Set 'em up!" he snapped at the boys on the fence.

CHAPTER EIGHT

Monday, June 20, 1880

The morning sun was already creating heat waves across the distant desert when Jeremiah reported to the Wells Fargo office. He was somewhat apprehensive about the upcoming experience, but also a bit proud of wearing his six-gun away from the practice area for the first time. A red-and-yellow stagecoach with its horses was parked in front of the office, two men working on it. Anita, in a long, dark-blue skirt and a white blouse with slightly ballooning sleeves and a collar that clung tightly to her neck, was standing on the boardwalk, observing the preparations.

"Good morning, Anita," Jeremiah said to the young woman, as he reached the office.

"Good morning, Jeremiah," Anita returned, smiling. She glanced at the wall clock through the window. "Quarter to eight; right on time. Wells Fargo likes that."

"Yes, m'am."

"Time for your first lesson," she said. "Come on, I'll introduce you to Herb." She led Jeremiah to the rear of the vehicle where a man was busily stowing luggage and packages in the rear boot.

"Herb," Anita said.

The man looked up. He was tall and lanky, even thin, with a slim face and an incongruously wide nose. Bushy eyebrows shaded blue eyes, a shaggy mustache hid his upper lip, and his black and gray locks fluffed out from underneath a floppy-brimmed, dark-brown hat. His countenance was cheerful.

"Herb," Anita repeated, "this is Jeremiah Bacon. Jeremiah, meet Herb Lambrecht."

"How do you do," Jeremiah said, extending a hand.

"Howdy, Jer," Herb said warmly, pumping his hand enthusiastically. "Anita says you're gonna be the new whip."

"Whip?"

"Drivers are called whips," Anita explained. "Or sometimes jehus."

"Yep," Herb confirmed. "And the drivin' is like the drivin' of Jehu, son of Mimshi; 'for he driveth furiously,' " he quoted with a big grin.

"That's the only Bible passage Herb knows, Jeremiah," Anita stated, smiling at the driver. "Herb, show him the stage and horses and introduce him to Seth. I'll go in to finish with the passengers."

"Sure thing, Anita," Herb said, throwing down the leather flap and securing it with straps.

Anita turned to Jeremiah. "You're in good hands, Jeremiah," she said. Jeremiah nodded, and Anita left for the office.

"There," Herb said as he finished buckling the last strap, "that oughta keep the dust out. C'mon, I'll have you meet Seth first."

The two men walked around the end of the coach and up to the team of horses. Three pairs of horses stood in front of the stage, some standing quietly, some chafing at their bits and fidgeting in their harnesses. A short, potbellied man wearing baggy pants held up by suspenders over a pair of dirty, faded, red long johns was adjusting the harness of one of the horses.

"Seth," Herb said as the two came up to the man. The man continued working as he turned his head. "This here's Jeremiah Bacon; he's gonna take Cyrus's place." Herb nodded toward the man. "Seth Miller."

"Morning," Jeremiah said.

"Mornin', fella," the man said without emotion. He

shook hands feebly and turned his attention back to his work.

"Not too talkative, Jer," Herb explained. "Particularly in the mornin'. He runs the Point of Rocks livery stable, and he's also stock tender for Wells Fargo. He looks after the stagecoach, too. We park it by his stable."

"I see."

"Know anything about harnesses?" Herb asked.

"No," Jeremiah admitted. "Will I have to harness the horses?"

"Sometimes, maybe," Herb said. "And you may have to unharness 'em at night. And who knows what can happen on the road." He turned to one of the horses. "The system's pretty simple really. Main part is the bellyband and backband, here and—here." He tugged at the leather straps that encircled the horse's body. Then he grabbed a horizontal leather strap. "These tugs or traces attach to the wiffletree back here and then extend up to the collar—up here, attached to the hames." He slapped the padded horse collar. "Horse gets a good push on this." He went to the horse's head. "You got your bridle up here and the reins are attached to it. Except for the leaders, the harness also has a neck-yoke strap which attaches the horse to the gooseneck part of the wagon tongue. And that's about it. The rest of these straps—this one and—here. Well, they're just sorta there to keep things in place."

Jeremiah looked doubtful. "Seems kind of complicated."

"You'll catch on," Herb said. He started back to the coach. "Ever ride in a coach like this before?"

"No."

"Well, this here's a Concord Coach from Concord, New Hampshire. Made by Abbot, Downing, and Company. It's eight feet high and five feet wide and weighs twenty-five hundred pounds. It's solid, well-built. Only the best wood, iron, and leather for the Concord. She could carry nine passengers inside alone, but we never get that many passengers so we just took out the middle seat to give the rest some more leg room."

Jeremiah examined the interior of the stagecoach. His determination of the previous day was shaken, and doubt was growing in his mind. Six big horses, a coach that weighed over a ton, passengers, and maybe a gold shipment. Not only did the job look more difficult than he'd considered, it also looked like it carried a lot more responsibility.

"Herb," Anita called from the office door, "the passengers are ready."

"Okay," he answered. Jeremiah followed him around to the stage door.

"Step right up, folks, plenty of room," Herb announced as he opened the door. "Make yourselves comfortable."

"Bull feathers." a man exclaimed. "Comfortable in one of these torture boxes?"

"Well, hi there, Vern," Herb greeted. "Back from Cheyenne already?"

"My sister don't live in a house, she lives in a museum. 'Don't sit here, don't sit there, don't touch that.' You can have the city." The man spat on the boardwalk contemptuously. "Take me back to my mine." He hopped into the stage.

"Jus' hold tight, Vern," Herb said. "We'll have you back to the diggin's in no time." Herb turned to the next passengers, a middle-aged couple. He tipped his hat to the woman. "Mornin', folks," he said cheerily.

"Good morning, driver," the man said. His wife smiled and nodded.

"Watch your step there, m'am," Herb cautioned, helping her in.

"Good morning, driver," a young woman said.

"Good mornin' to you, m'am," Herb returned, again

tipping his hat. He extended his hand as she stepped up toward the coach. "Allow me."

"Thank you."

"Any more?" Herb asked Anita as she came out of the office.

"No. Vern's going to South Pass City; the others are going to Lander." She handed him a canvas bag. "Here's the mail sack. The strong box is ready, too."

"Okay," Herb said. He turned to Jeremiah. "Here, stick this in the front boot."

"Where's that?" Jeremiah asked.

"Under the driver's seat, of course," Herb said, smiling at the ignorance of his new apprentice. He went into the office as Jeremiah swung the bag into the boot. Herb returned carrying a green strong box, which was thrown into the front boot, also.

"Hop up there, Jer," Herb said. "Left side."

Jeremiah climbed up to the driver's seat and took a position on the left side. Herb ascended in a bound, settled himself on the right, and grabbed the three pairs of reins that were wrapped around the brake handle. The horses started to prance and jingle in their harnesses.

"Eager critters, aren't they?" Herb commented. "Now," he said, leaning toward Jeremiah and speaking softly. "First lesson is appearance. Make it look like the most important thing to you in the world is gettin' your passengers to their destinations as quick as possible. And particularly for folks like them that just got off the train, we got to show 'em that we think we're as fast as any train. So always gallop outa town and into town. Looks good."

Jeremiah nodded, paying close attention. He glanced nervously at Anita, who smiled up at him. Seth was standing on the ground near her with a bored expression on his face.

Herb raised a hand in farewell.

"Have a good trip," Anita called from the boardwalk.

Herb disengaged the brake with his foot, snapped the reins, and let out a loud cry of "Heeyah!" Jeremiah was startled at the volume of the call, coming as it did from the wiry man.

All six horses burst into action, straining against their collars. Rings, buckles, snaps, and chain links all clinked loudly as the harness gear came taut. The team shot forward, and the stage lurched, swaying backward on its thoroughbraces. Jeremiah looked back at Anita again as he grabbed for the iron handrail and hung on tightly. Anita waved to him, and he managed a weak smile.

The stage raced through the short main street of Point of Rocks. A cloud of dust rose from the horses' hooves, and a stream of like material spun off of each wheel. A few boys scattered from the path of the stage as it tore past.

The stage headed east out of Point of Rocks, paralleling the same gray cliffs and bluffs that formed a backdrop for the town. The rock formations became increasingly stratified with layers of tan and finally were completely displaced by worn hills of rocky, brown earth.

Herb slowed the team and guided the horses up one of the gentle hills and headed the stage northward. The countryside here was flatter and more open, with bare soil supporting some scattered clumps of grass but mostly gray-green sagebrush and light-green greasewood.

Pronghorn antelope looked up from their grazing to stare at the passing stage. Horned larks flew up from the path of the horses, and a ground squirrel watched while sitting on its haunches.

The stage swayed and rocked like a boat in a rough sea as the horses drew it over what was optimistically called a road. Sometimes the iron tires would hit a particularly large rock, causing the stage to tip up at a crazy angle, and Jeremiah felt sure they would

tip over completely. But the stage always jolted upright again.

"Okay, Jer," Herb said, "now that you're used to
the ride—"

"I am?"

Herb laughed. "After a while the stage will be like
part of your own body. You'll see. Anyway, let me
show you the reins. Those for turnin' left you keep in
your left hand, those for turnin' right in your right
hand."

"Makes sense."

"Okay. Now the reins of the leaders you keep—"

"The leaders are the ones up front?" Jeremiah
asked.

"Right. They're the smartest horses. The next span
is the swing team, and the big fellas right in front of
us are the wheelers."

"Okay."

"By the way, horses on the right are on the off side,
and those on the left are on the near side."

"How come?" Jeremiah asked. "Seems backwards."

Herb shrugged his shoulders. "Hell, I don't know
Jeremiah nodded.

"Gettin' back to what I was sayin', you keep the
reins of the leaders between your fore and middle
fingers, the swingers' reins between your middle and
third fingers, and the wheelers' between the third
and little fingers."

"Got it—I think."

"Good. Now don't pull too tight nor too loose. You
always want to 'feel' the horses' mouths. Too tight
and a horse gets calluses, doesn't respond, gets 'cold-
mouthed.' You want to keep him 'sweet.' "

Jeremiah nodded again.

"And these horses," Herb continued, "usually go
over the same road again and again. So they get to
know it. You don't have to keep on 'em for every
little twist of the road. 'Cept when you get a new
team. A lot of this horseflesh is mustang, straight off

the Great Divide Basin, and they need constant watch-in' 'til they get the hang of it."

"What about the whip?" Jeremiah asked, pointing to the device at Herb's right.

"Never use it," Herb informed him. "I like to talk to the horses through the ribbons." He hefted the reins.

Jeremiah took a deep breath. "I hope I can remember all this."

"You'll get the hang of it, jus' like the horses," Herb encouraged. "Jus' a little practice. You watch me closely the rest of the trip."

"Yes, sir."

The stage continued more or less northward through land that was a monotony of sagebrush, greasewood, and bare earth with snatches of grass. The sun was directly overhead; the hills to the west and the mountains to the north shimmered in the distant heat waves. A golden eagle soared effortlessly on thermals rising from the desert floor.

Jeremiah shifted in his seat trying to get comfortable. His buttocks hurt from the jostling, his left hand was stiff from clutching the handrail, and his back pained him from the constant twisting. Sweat tried to drip off his nose but was arrested by the dust rising up from the road and floating into his face. His shirt stuck to his back, his pants clung to him, and his feet roasted in their boots.

"You like driving a stage, Herb?" Jeremiah asked in his misery.

"Sure," the man answered. "Pay's not bad, and it's regular."

"Mm. Get a chance to talk to the passengers much?"

"Some at meals, but if I see a particularly interestin' fellow, I ask him to sit up here with me. Sittin' with the driver is an honor, you know."

Jeremiah looked down from the top of the swaying stagecoach at the wheels and horses' hooves throwing up a cloud of dust, sand, and pebbles. "No," he said, "I didn't know that."

"Yep. A whip's not jus' a stone sittin' up here. He's a man of responsibility. Gotta be skilled, honorable, congenial. Think of the best interests of his passengers." His eyes brightened. "Say, you ever hear of Hank Monk?"

"No."

"The most famous stage driver of all time?" Herb asked, incredulous.

"No," Jeremiah said.

"Well, you've heard of Horace Greeley, haven't you?"

"Of course."

"Well, let me tell you about Hank Monk and Horace Greeley," Herb said, delighted at another opportunity to tell his favorite story. "Hank Monk was the driver from Carson City to Placerville at the time ol' Horace Greeley was passin' through in fifty-nine. Well, when the two of 'em left Carson City, Hank had been hittin' the bottle, and Horace wasn't real sure he'd get to Placerville in good time. He says to Monk, 'Driver, I've got to be in Placerville for an appointment, and I think we're gonna be late.' Now, Hank Monk never let a passenger down in his life, and he was never late. So he says, 'Hang on, Mr. Greeley. I'll get you through on time.' Well," Herb said slowly, pausing to chuckle, "Hank drove that stage along those mountain roads like he was late for his own funeral. Up, down, turn, and twist, rough road and all, right across the Sierras, top speed all the way. It's a wonder ol' Horace weren't killed what with all the bouncin' 'round inside that coach. But they got to Placerville on time." Herb laughed and slapped his thigh.

Jeremiah couldn't quite see the humor in it that Herb did, but he laughed good-humoredly. "That's a good one, Herb," he said. He shifted his weight to relieve a sore spot. "You always been a stage driver, Herb?"

"No," Herb answered. "Before the war I was on a farm in Carolina."

"Carolina?" Jeremiah repeated in surprise.

"Yep. Spent four years defendin' the state, but left after the war. Couldn't stand to live in a place crawlin' with carpetbaggers and bluebellies."

"To come to Point of Rocks?" Jeremiah asked disbelievingly.

"Not directly," Herb said. "Bummed for a while, then punched cattle. Drove a stage on the Overland Route from Green River to Fort Bridger—they're west o' here—then went up to the South Pass area late in sixty-seven to make my fortune in gold." A big smile grew across Herb's face.

"Did you find gold?"

"Sure did," Herb said triumphantly. "Spent most of it as fast as I found it, though." There was no sign of regret in his voice. "But the strikes never did amount to much. I stayed a year, then got back my old job drivin' the stage. But the Union Pacific reached the western edge of Wyoming by the end of the year, and by the end of the next it reached clear across the continent. Well, that shot the hell outa the transcontinental stage business. I was lucky enough to get this job."

"Anita said you also ranched."

"Yep. I didn't spend all that gold. So when I got hitched to a pretty young thing from Green River, I bought me a little spread south o' Bitter Creek. It's not much. Couldn't make a go of it without this stage drivin'."

"It amazes me that anybody makes a go of it in this kind of country—or wants to."

Herb laughed. "Well," he observed, scanning the scenery, "it's hard country all right, but it grows on you after a while. You'll see." He looked at Jeremiah "You'll see."

Jeremiah happened to look down into the boot "Say, isn't that a Winchester rifle?"

"Carbine," Herb corrected. "Any good with one?"

"Never fired one."

"What? Hell of a lot o' good you're gonna be as a 'shotgun.' Try it."

"Okay." Jeremiah reached into the boot and grabbed the carbine. He hefted in in his hands and then pointed it at a bush. He cocked the hammer, then pulled the trigger. The shot rang out.

"What's up, Herb?" Vern called from inside the stage.

"Jus' some target practice, Vern," Herb reassured him. He noticed Jeremiah rubbing his shoulder "You've got to hold the gun tight against your shoulder so the kick pushes your shoulder back 'stead of hittin' it. Try again."

Hesitantly Jeremiah pulled down on the carbine s lever. A cartridge, trailed by a wisp of smoke, popped out of the breech. He returned the lever to its original position and noticed that the hammer was cocked already. Holding the butt tight against his shoulder he took another shot at a bush. The kick was considerably diminished. He fired the carbine twice more and then reached to put it away.

"It shoots nice, Herb."

"I like it," Herb said. "But replace the cartridges you used before you put it away. There's a box of shells in the boot."

Jeremiah recalled the marshal's similar advice. He retrieved a box of cartridges from the boot and clumsily managed to slip four shells into the magazine through the loading port on the right side of the receiver. Then he put the carbine and box back into the boot.

*   *

"You gettin' hungry, Jer?" Herb asked.

"I'm famished," Jeremiah replied. His stomach had been growling for some time.

"Lunch is jus' ahead," Herb said, nodding in that direction.

"Trees!" Jeremiah exclaimed.

Herb laughed. "Yep. Morrow Creek swing station. Fresh horses, a meal, and some water."

Jeremiah's face broke out into a wide grin, his spirits rising. He couldn't remember a meal being so welcome.

Herb drove the stage into the yard of the station, put his foot to the brake, and brought the team to a noisy halt in front of a man and woman waiting in front of their small adobe house. There were two corrals in back, and another building used as a barn. Morrow Creek was barely a trickle, but it gave enough water to support some willows and cottonwood trees.

"Hello, Barney," Herb called from the stage, as he struggled with the horses, which were unable to calm down immediately after their long run.

"Herb," the station manager greeted, with a wave of his hand.

Herb wrapped the reins around the brake handle and jumped down from his perch. Jeremiah wearily climbed down from his side and stood gratefully on the solid ground. He stretched himself on his toes, reached toward the sky, and strained his muscles. Then he relaxed and shook himself. Still, he couldn't seem to throw the feeling that he was still moving.

"Barney Wilson," Herb said to the station manager, "meet Jeremiah Bacon. He's gonna be takin' the Monday run after this."

"Glad to meet you, Jeremiah," Barney said.

"How do you do," Jeremiah returned, and shook hands with the man.

"Morrow Creek, folks," Herb shouted, opening the stage door. "Time to stretch your legs and put some food in your bellies. Outhouse in back." He extended a hand to the younger woman as she alighted from the stage.

"Enjoyin' the trip so far, m'am?"

"Well, at least it's getting me closer to my husband."

"Yes, m'am."

The other passengers followed her out, and they all headed eagerly for the door of the building, led by the station manager's wife.

"You two better get yourselves in there, too, and get some grub," Barney warned. "Won't last long."

Inside the one-roomed building Jeremiah found a large wooden table spread with a surprising array of food between the rows of plates and utensils. The passengers were already eating, and Mrs. Wilson was busy placing more food on the table and pouring coffee, keeping up a pleasant chatter all the while.

Herb and Jeremiah sat down also and dug in. Roast antelope, fried potatoes, canned tomatoes, warm rolls, butter, peas, raw onions, applesauce, and a pie. The meal was over too soon for Jeremiah; he would have enjoyed sitting around a good deal longer.

Jeremiah joined Herb in helping Barney hitch up the fresh team. The reluctant passengers straggled back to the stagecoach, and Herb, ever solicitous, helped them get in. After closing the door, he joined Jeremiah on the driver's seat.

With a fresh team of horses straining at the harness, the stage surged away from the station, immediately setting Jeremiah's sore muscles to aching again. He waved to the Wilsons, and they waved back heartily.

"You ever been held up, Herb?" Jeremiah asked.

"Yep," he answered, "six times, and Cyrus was held up over a dozen times durin' the last couple o' years."

"The Red Desert Gang?"

"Yep, and each time it happens the same way. Same fellow in a duster and hood sits on his horse blockin' the road, and the rest of the gang keeps you covered from ridges. Not a chance to do anything."

"Did you recognize the man on the horse?"

"Naw," Herb said. "Can't see anything through that hood. But he's got a funny voice. Kinda deep and scratchy."

"Why, that sounds like the leader of the men who killed my father," Jeremiah exclaimed.

"Not surprisin'. He seems to be the fellow in charge in all the holdups," Herb observed. "But he's not the real headman," he pointed out. "Somebody else is on top, somebody in Point of Rocks."

"How do you know that?"

"The gang gets information from town, there's no other way they could know about the timin' of the gold shipments."

"Oh. Well, but—couldn't it be somebody from the mines?" Jeremiah suggested.

"Can't be," Herb insisted. "Any shipment comin' from the mines that we don't know about ahead of time gets through. And take the night your pa was killed. That's only the second time that a shipment has been robbed some place other than on the stage. Nobody in Atlantic City knew those greenbacks and coins had come in on the train, and even more important, no one knew that on Thursday we were plannin' a trap for 'em."

"A trap?"

"Yep. Cyrus was gonna drive, but MacKenzie, Warner, and me were gonna ride a ways behind him. If the stage got held up, we'd catch the whole gang in the act—or do some thinnin', at least. But the gang knew," Herb emphasized. "They knew about the trap, so they robbed the office instead. No way they coulda found out about that from anywhere except in Point of Rocks."

"Well, who told?"

"Hell," Herb sputtered, "if we knew that we woulda done somethin' about it!"

"Yes, stupid of me," Jeremiah said.

"That's the damn riddle," Herb said solemnly. "Who could be tellin' 'em? I jus' can't figure it out. Hardly anyone knew. Me, the marshal, his deputy, Cyrus, and Anita. That's all. So who told?"

"And you've never noticed the guy with the funny voice in town?"

"Never," Herb said. "Cyrus and I've never come across him, and that voice is different enough that even MacKenzie or Warner could spot it from jus' our description. No, someone else is gettin' the information from either the Wells Fargo office or the marshal's office and gettin' it out to that guy. But I can't figure out who's tellin'. I'd trust my life to the marshal or his deputy. I know it ain't me. And Cyrus is dead now; I know it wasn't him, anyway. And Anita—well, I'm ashamed to even think o' her."

Jeremiah pondered the perplexing situation for a moment. "Have there been other stage robbers besides the Red Desert Gang?"

"Oh, one or two in the early days of the gold rush in the South Pass area, but the Red Desert Gang's the only bunch that's been 'round since then. And they've only been here the last couple o' years. They've had the business all to themselves. Not much gold comes out of the mines in the South Pass area anymore, but havin' inside information they can be sure of haulin in enough to keep it worthwhile."

"Anyone else besides Kessler and my father been hurt in a holdup?"

"Oh, sure," Herb said. "One of my shotgun messen gers was wounded once. Tried to fight it out after they already had the drop on him."

"I'll make sure to get the drop first."

"You be real careful," Herb cautioned. "A deputy of MacKenzie's was killed about a year-and-a-half ago, too. And Anita's mother was killed in a holdup back at the office, the only other time it's been held up."

"My God!" Jeremiah gasped. "Anita's been—the

tragedy she's—" He was in anguish for the young woman.

"Damn fine woman, that Anita," Herb said. "If I were your age again and single I'd be thinkin' 'bout corralin' that young filly," he added and nudged Jeremiah's shoulder as he winked at him.

"Aww," Jeremiah scoffed, but he had to admit that the thought was not unpleasant.

"Say," he said, returning to the subject of holdups, "how come you can't get an escort from the mines to protect the shipments? The mining companies must be losing a lot of money."

"Oh, no," Herb corrected. "The customers never lose a cent; Wells Fargo makes good any losses. It's their bond of faith with the shippers. That's why the stage company's so hot to get this Red Desert Gang. They've lost a heap o' money by now. They're offerin' fifty dollars apiece for any member o' the gang and five hundred for the leader."

"I could use that money," Jeremiah declared.

"Gettin' it might be kind of hard," Herb pointed out.

The land changed a bit, becoming more hilly. The vegetation became sparser, the sagebrush smaller, exposing large patches of reddish, gravelly soil. The twisting road followed a wide valley through barren hills. Jeremiah was fascinated to see melting banks of snow still clinging to the hillsides in sheltered spots.

It was evening when the stage left the valley and came within sight of a river coursing through low hills that marched off to a magnificent range of snow-capped peaks.

"Sweetwater River station," Herb informed Jeremiah. "Look at all that lovely water."

The stage pulled up in front of a building of unfinished wood, the planks nailed vertically to form walls. A small wooden shed served for storage, and a corral completed the setup. A man stood resting his arms on the backs of the two wheelers in the fresh team of horses that was waiting, all harnessed, the swing pole suspended between the middle span.

"Evenin', Leon," Herb called with a wave of his hand as he steadied the team.

The other man waved and then approached the stage.

Herb leaped down and went to the stage door as Jeremiah crawled down from his seat, again thankful for the solid earth and the chance to loosen up his stiff muscles.

"All out for the Sweetwater River swing station, folks. Good water to wash the dust outa your throats, and outhouses for the call o' nature."

The passengers descended wearily from the coach and made their way toward the building. "Ten minutes," Herb called after them.

"Hey, Leon," he said, walking up to the stock-tender, who was now unhitching the exhausted team. "Meet Jeremiah Bacon, new whip for the Monday run."

"How do you do," Jeremiah said, offering his hand.

" 'Lo," the man responded, giving Jeremiah's hand a single vigorous pump.

"Let's get ourselves a drink, Jer," Herb said, and headed for the river. Jeremiah tagged along eagerly.

Here finally was a river worthy of the name. It was fifty feet wide and three feet deep. Cold, clear, and fast, making pleasant gurgling noises among the rocks and willows bordering the shore. Lush green grass and shrubs spread away from the river for a short distance, stopping abruptly where the hills began, the latter showing only the same scattered, struggling vegetation as before.

Herb tossed his hat aside, lay facedown on the grass, and stuck his head under the water. He came up shaking like a grizzly and wiped the excess water from his face with his hands. The water dripped off his hair and ran in rivulets down the back of his vest.

Jeremiah whipped off his hat and followed Herb's lead. The icy water shocked his face and sent a welcome chill down his back. He came up sputtering and gasping for air.

"Damn good, ain't it?" Herb commented.

"Beautiful!"

Herb cupped a hand and scooped up some water. He slurped up the cold liquid, then shook his hand, sighed in satisfaction, and sat back on the grass.

Jeremiah needed no coaxing, and he had a long drink himself. He sat next to Herb and gazed about at the panorama before him. "Gee, this is a pretty place," he said. "The river, the mountains."

"Those are the Wind River Mountains to the northwest," Herb said. "That's where this water comes from. In back of us is the Sweetwater range." He took a deep breath and let it out slowly. "Yep, a mighty pretty spot. Was used as a swing station on the early Overland Stage Route."

"No kidding."

"Yep. And the Oregon and California Trails crossed the river right here." Herb pointed a finger at the ground.

"Really?"

"Yep. Back in the forties and fifties a couple o' hundred-thousand people rode or walked right over this very ground. 'Bout ten miles to the southwest is South Pass itself, the easiest place in the Rocky Mountains for a wagon to cross. Pass is twenty miles wide with jus' gentle rollin' hills. Lot o' people didn't even know they were in a pass 'til they'd crossed it already. And a couple o' miles past South Pass is Pacific Springs, with plenty of water and grass. Its waters go to the Pacific; that's how it got its name. This water," he said, nodding to the Sweetwater River, "goes to the Atlantic."

"Herb," Leon called from behind them, interrupting.

"Okay, Leon," Herb acknowledged, grabbing his hat. He rose to his feet. "Let's hit the road, Jer."

They returned to the stage and helped the last of the passengers back into the coach. Herb mounted the box and gathered in the reins. He waited for the reluctant Jeremiah to take his place, then gave Leon a salute, and set the team into motion, but not at the usual, frenzied pace.

Herb slowed the team even more at the water's edge and then urged them into the stream. Jeremiah gazed into the clear water and watched the dust wash off the wheels and float away. Once out of the water, a fine spray flew off the wheels as the stage gathered speed, but it quickly stopped, trapped by the dust of the road.

The team took the stagecoach over foothills and gray-green ridges, through land surrounded by buttes, mountains, and hills, with scattered vegetation, mostly scrubby grass and sage, but also some pine trees showing in the distance on the hills in some gullies. The sun, almost out of sight now, washed the sky with brilliant reds and purples.

"Hey," Jeremiah said, pointing ahead. "There's a big building!"

"Yep," Herb said. "The Carissa mine at South Pass City."

Jeremiah glanced around. "I don't see any town."

"You will. See that cemetery on the hill ahead?"

"Yes, I see it."

"Town's right behind it."

Jeremiah looked doubtful, but he realized that Herb must know the location. The stage drew near to the iron fence-enclosed cemetery, and suddenly Jeremiah could see buildings in the gulch beyond the cemetery.

Herb put the horses into a gallop just as they reached the hill leading down to the town. The stage hurtled down the slope, and the entire town now came into view The horses swung to the left, and the stage swayed sharply to the right.

"Herb!" Jeremiah cried, sure they were going to tip over. But Herb simply urged the horses on more. They took that curve, raced past some buildings, and then turned sharply to the right, entering the main street. The stage tilted precariously over to the left this time, and Jeremiah hung on with desperation and fear.

Herb jammed on the foot brake and pulled back hard on the reins. "Whoa! Whoa!" The stage came to a lurching halt, with the stage door aligned precisely with the door of a hotel.

"South Pass City, folks," Herb called down. "Jer, open up the rear boot and get the luggage."

Jeremiah sighed gratefully and uncurled his stiffened hand from the handrail. "Okay," he said. He climbed down from the box, relieved that the ride was over for the day. He went to the back of the stage and unfastened the straps, then started to pile the luggage on the boardwalk.

"Dinner and overnight accommodations," Herb said, opening the stage door.

The miner was the first out.

"Ride with us again, Vern," Herb encouraged.

"God save me," Vern responded. He went to the luggage, picked out a carpetbag, and then headed down the street.

"Evening, Herb," a man said, coming out of the door of the hotel.

"Evenin', Eldon," Herb returned. "Got some customers for you."

"Good, good," the man replied.

Herb extended his hand to the young wife as she stepped down, and Eldon rushed up to offer his assistance. "Allow me, m'am," he said, stealing her hand from Herb's and leading her toward the hotel door. "Step right into the lobby, m'am, and we'll have you set up comfortably in an instant."

"Thank you, sir," she said, smiling.

Herb helped the couple for Lander out of the stage and watched them follow Eldon and his charge into the hotel. He came back to help Jeremiah. "I would have introduced you right away, but Eldon was busy."

"So I saw."

"He's the hotel owner and Wells Fargo agent in South Pass City," Herb told Jeremiah. "He's also the general store owner, postmaster, part time miner, and part owner of the only saloon left in town—right next to the hotel. Let's get this stuff inside."

In two trips Herb and Jeremiah had deposited the luggage, the mail pouch, and the strong box in the hotel lobby, ready for Eldon's disposition. After that Herb, accompanied by Jeremiah, drove the stage down the street to the blacksmith's shop. They parked the stage behind it, and released the horses into a corral after unharnessing them. Hay and water had already been provided. Then they returned to the hotel.

Inside, the lobby was off to the left and a hallway led straight ahead, as did a narrow stairway leading to the second floor. To the right was the dining room, filled with square tables covered with red and white checkered tablecloths and surrounded by four chairs. The pleasant and enticing smell of hot food wafted in from the kitchen to the rear, and Jeremiah's mouth watered. He and Herb sat at one of the tables.

Eldon had seated all of the passengers at a single table and joined them himself. He kept up a more or less one-sided conversation with them; the travelers were too busy eating to talk, satisfying a hunger that only a grueling stage ride on a hot desert could impart.

After supper, Herb and Jeremiah left the hotel. They sauntered along, enjoying the cool night air.

The town was little more than one dusty street, perhaps half a mile long. There were clapboard buildings, dugouts along the hills, barns, false-front stores, and sundry other buildings and homes, most of them obviously deserted and fallen into disrepair or actually collapsing. Small, fast Willow Creek ran along the south side of the town. The hills started right at the backs of the buildings on the north and at the banks of the creek on the south, and they closed off both ends of the main street, except for a small side-gulch, also crammed full of dilapidated buildings, on the west end of town.

Few lights glowed in the town. The abandoned buildings presented only vague shapes in the darkness or ghostly silhouettes against a sky strewn with stars.

"It's kind of spooky," Jeremiah said, "all these buildings and yet so few people."

"It ain't much to look at now, Jer," Herb said, "but back in sixty-seven and early sixty-eight this place was really boomin', jammed packed with people. Hotels, bakeries, meat markets, breweries, and you couldn't count the saloons or whorehouses. And there were stamp mills for processin' ore, a sawmill for lumber from the Wind River Mountains, doctors, a newspaper—you name it."

They started back for the hotel. "You really liked it here then, I guess," Jeremiah said, detecting the pleasure in Herb's voice at recalling the early town.

"Ah, that was the life, Jer," Herb said. "Excitin', raw, wild. Gold flowin' all over, money, liquor, women, gamblin', work hard all day and play hard all night. I had myself one hell of a time."

Herb turned in at the saloon next to the hotel, and Jeremiah followed him in.

"What are you drinkin', Jer?" Herb asked. "I'm buyin'."

"A beer will do," Jeremiah said. He didn't really

want one, but he'd learned his lesson at the Bitter Creek well.

"Billy," Herb called to the bartender as he pulled a chair away from a table, "a bottle for me and a beer for my partner here." He sat down, and Jeremiah sat in a chair next to him. The bartender brought over a mug of beer as well as a whiskey bottle with a glass perched upside down on top of it.

"Billy Morrison, meet Jeremiah Bacon, new whip for the stage," Herb said. "Jer, Billy here's part owner of the saloon along with Eldon."

"Evening," Jeremiah said, shaking hands with the bartender.

"Glad to meet ya, Jeremiah," Billy said. Then he walked back to the bar.

Herb popped the cork on the bottle and poured some of the liquor into his glass. Jeremiah took a sip of the beer and set the mug back down on the table. He took a look around the saloon. It was smaller than the Bitter Creek. A long bar filled most of the east wall. Stocks of liquor, a large mirror, and a stuffed deer's head decorated the wall itself. At the back of the saloon was a small, raised stage in the left-hand corner with—amazing!—a piano standing on it. A potbellied stove with a supply of firewood stacked next to it was situated between the stage and a door. The west wall had two windows and a stuffed antelope's head. Four round tables were scattered throughout the room. Herb, the bartender, and he were the only occupants of the saloon.

"This whole town is kind of depressing, Herb," Jeremiah said.

Herb glanced around, stared at Jeremiah a moment, and then downed the drink in a single gulp. He wiped his lips on his shirt sleeve. "May still get a few customers, but I know what you mean. This town once was alive, growin', throbbin'. Now—almost dead." He poured himself another drink. "Point of Rocks could be like this in a little while."

Jeremiah looked intently at the stage driver. "How so?"

"The gold may give out completely here and in Atlantic City, and even if it doesn't, Wells Fargo may call it quits with the stage line if the robberies keep up. The line can't survive on jus' mail and passengers." Herb gulped down the second drink and poured another. "The few ranches around Point of Rocks wouldn't be put out much to have to go to Rock Springs or even Green River for supplies. And without the gold mines, there'd be little reason for the railroad to stop in Point of Rocks. After that, there'd be no reason at all for the town to exist anymore."

"You make it sound pretty bleak."

"No stage, no job. I could wind up diggin' in the coal mines at Rock Springs. And that, Jer, scares the hell outa me." The third drink went down his throat.

Jeremiah looked down at his hands. They already looked the worse for wear, and he hadn't even done any of the driving yet. And would he wind up digging coal along with Herb if he stayed in Point of Rocks? What shape would his hands be in then? Callused, bruised, battered, all sensation gone from the fingers. He wouldn't be able to feel the piano keys.

"Hey, Jer," Herb interrupted, as if reading Jeremiah's thoughts. "How 'bout playin' a little somethin' for us?" he suggested, trying to change the mood.

Jeremiah glanced at the piano and considered it. This piano did look better than the one in the Bitter Creek, but he was exhausted from the stage ride. "I don't think I could manage to walk over to it, much less play a tune, Herb," he said. "I'm beat."

"Hm. Well, how 'bout some poker with Billy and me?"

"I don't know how to play, and—'

"We'll teach you."

"—I really think I ought to go to bed. Tomorrow's going to be here before I'll be ready for it."

Herb laughed. "You'll get hardened, I promise you."

"Where do we sleep, anyway?"

"Hotel," Herb informed him. "Last room on the right, upstairs. Only one bed; we'll have to share. Hope that won't bother you."

"It wouldn't bother me if one of the horses climbed in, Herb. I'm going to sleep like a rock."

Herb laughed again. "See you in the mornin', Jer."

"Good night, Herb," Jeremiah said, rising from his chair.

CHAPTER NINE

Tuesday, June 21, 1880

At eight o'clock sharp the stage bolted from in front of the hotel and raced down the dusty main street of South Pass City. The passengers seemed already exhausted from anticipation of the rough ride ahead, and Jeremiah wished he were back in Point of Rocks. Only Herb seemed to be enjoying himself.

The horses followed a road that climbed out of town heading north, past the Carissa mine buildings. They pulled the stage across a series of bare sagebrush hills and gulches. Old mine structures and holes dug by hopeful prospectors in the hard shale studded these gulches, and light-green pine, aspen, and willow bordered a small stream.

It took only a few minutes to reach Atlantic City. This town showed much more activity than South Pass City, but it was obvious that it, too, had declined from a bygone boom era.

Herb galloped the team down the main street, scattering some pedestrians, and pulled the horses expertly to a sudden stop in front of a hotel. A man holding a small packet of letters in his hand was standing in the street in front of the hotel.

"Morning, Herb," the man said. He tossed the letters up to the driver.

"Howdy, Homer," Herb said, reaching for the mail-pouch in the boot. "Homer, this here's Jeremiah Bacon. He'll be takin' the Monday run." He put the letters into the pouch.

"Morning, Jeremiah," Homer greeted.

"Morning," Jeremiah returned.

Herb pulled a packet of letters, secured with a string, from the pouch. "Mail for you, Homer."

"Thanks." Homer glanced at the letters. "Oh, by the way," he added, taking a note from his shirt pocket, "for Anita."

Herb took the note. "Anythin' else?"

"Nope. See you this afternoon."

"So long, Homer."

Jeremiah waved as Herb again set the horses into a gallop, the stage swaying back on its thoroughbraces. They raced down the street and were quickly out of town.

The road continued through gulches and over hills, continually rising. Pines and aspens became quite thick, closing in on the stage as it wound its way toward the summit of the range of hills. In the open spaces wild flowers bloomed in profusion. Then it was downhill, requiring frequent braking to prevent the coach from overtaking the horses on the narrow road cut into the shoulders of the wooden slopes. Into a wide valley the road paralleled a river, the Little Popo Agie, on one side and on the other side high, red cliffs. The valley broadened to form a hilly plain, which had pastures with cattle and fields of planted crops forming a cover of green that contrasted with the red soil.

The stage had a brief ten-minute stop for a fresh team at a ranch that served as the Little Popo Agie swing station. Shortly past noon they pulled into Lander, a small town on the banks of the Popo Agie River.

Again Herb displayed his skill with the team, stopping the stage perfectly in front of the Wells Fargo office. He was quick to jump down and help the passengers out with a call of "Lander! Connections for Fort Washakie, Riverton, Shoshone, Thermopolis, and Montana."

The young woman passenger stepped down into the street and looked around expectantly.

"Luella!" someone called.

"Steve!" she answered excitedly.

Jeremiah looked down the boardwalk and saw a young cavalry officer, one hand on his scabbard and the other waving enthusiastically in the air, running toward the stage. His wife ran to meet him, and the couple fell into an immediate and prolonged embrace.

"Isn't that sweet," the other woman passenger commented to her husband as she stepped off the stage herself.

"Mm," her husband said apathetically. They both went into the office.

The young officer and his wife returned to the stage, arm in arm. Herb and Jeremiah quickly removed luggage from the rear boot and placed it on the boardwalk. The officer picked up his wife's bags and marched off down the boardwalk, nodding to his wife's constant narrative.

The rest of the luggage and freight was taken into the office. Herb introduced Jeremiah to the Wells Fargo agent in Lander and also delivered the last of the mail. Then they drove the stage over to the livery stable, where a fresh team would be harnessed. Herb and Jeremiah did take the time to have a quick lunch at a nearby restaurant.

A little before one, Herb drove the stage to the stage office, and the mailpouch, with its new contents, was tossed back into the front boot. A few freight packages for South Pass City were added, but there were no passengers. Herb climbed down and walked around the stage and ascended the left side.

"Move over, Jer," he said. "Time for you to drive. With an empty stage you can only kill the two of us." He laughed.

"I think I ought to watch you a little more," Jeremiah suggested nervously.

"Naw," Herb rejected. "Best way to learn is to jus' go ahead and try it."

With trepidation Jeremiah slid over to the right side of the driver's seat. "Do you have any gloves?" he asked.

"What for?" Herb replied.

"I'd like to protect my hands." Jeremiah's scalp cringed as he noticed Herb's cheerful countenance suddenly go grim.

"I never use gloves myself," Herb said. "Deadens the touch." He stared at Jeremiah a moment. "Look, kid," he said. "It's none of my business. You're your own man. But if you mean to stay in this country, you're gonna have to stop being so prissy concerned about your hands. I'm willin' as the next man to help you out, particularly since Anita seems so set up on it, but if you're not willin' to get your hands dirty, you might as well climb down from this seat right now and make the rest of the trip inside the coach."

Jeremiah gulped. He nodded slowly. "I'm staying up here," he said.

A smile returned to Herb's face. "Good man," he said.

Carefully Jeremiah inserted the reins from the various spans between the proper fingers as he had seen Herb do so often. He put his foot gently on the brake handle and looked at Herb.

Herb checked Jeremiah's grip and nodded. "Let's go."

Jeremiah released the brake, flicked the reins, and gave a "Yeh!" to the horses. Several of the horses lunged at their harnesses, others took hesitant steps, and one of the leaders didn't move at all. The stage jolted forward and then rocked backward again. The horses set the harnesses rattling, and the leather straps cracked as they snapped taut and then slackened again.

"Whoa!" Herb yelled. "Hit the brake."

Jeremiah awkwardly shot his foot out for the brake handle, but he missed and had to aim again. He pulled back hard on the reins at the same time, and all the horses stopped moving.

"What was all that?" Herb asked.

"I—to start . . ."

"Oh, I thought you sneezed."

Jeremiah fidgeted in his seat, embarrassed.

"Try it again, Jer," Herb said. "And this time let the horses know you really want to start."

"Yes, sir," Jeremiah said. He wiped the perspiration off his hands onto his pants legs and then seized the reins once more. He concentrated for a moment, then gave the reins a vigorous snap and hollered at the top of his lungs. "Hi yah!"

"Atta boy, Jer," Herb cheered, slapping him on the shoulder as the team bolted forward and the coach swung back. Jeremiah was amazed at how much faster the horses seemed to move when he was actually holding the reins.

"Pass that wagon comin' toward us on the right. Turn 'em all as a unit."

Jeremiah glanced at the wagon and single span of horses coming toward them down the street, and he judged there would be plenty of room to pass. He gave a tug on the right reins. Then, surprised at how fast the two teams were closing, he tugged a little harder.

"Not too far," Herb warned. Jeremiah slackened the right reins and tugged on the left ones to pull the team back.

"You're overcorrectin', Jer," Herb shouted. "Stop 'em!" he called urgently, and reached involuntarily for the reins. "The brake!"

Jeremiah lunged for the brake handle and missed again. It was too late. The leaders crashed into the oncoming team. Horses reared and whinnied, and harness leather, metal rings, and buckles clacked against each other. The two teams were locked in a thrashing tumult, and frightened, angry cries issued from the animals.

Herb was off the box in a flash, but the other driver let loose with a string of profanities, casting aspersions on Jeremiah's family, his ancestors and descendants, and all the horses and mules in his hometown. However, Herb quickly had the horses calmed and separated. He walked around to the driver of the wagon and spoke a few words, but the only result was that the man then directed his tirade at Herb.

Herb came back to the stage and climbed up. "No damage done, Jer," he said. "Nasty-tempered fellow, ain't he?"

"Herb," Jeremiah pleaded, "you take over."

"Nonsense," the man said. "You gotta learn somehow."

Jeremiah looked down at the people who had gathered on the boardwalk nearby and were staring at him. His embarrassment grew.

"Have at 'em, Jer," Herb said cheerfully. He tipped his hat to the man in the wagon and smiled as the fellow drove past. "Nice to meet you," he said sarcastically. "Hope we run into you again sometime."

Jeremiah took a deep breath and set the horses in motion again, but his shout and rein-handling were even less confident than the first time. Holding the reins gave him an entirely new perspective on sitting on top of a racing stagecoach.

"We turn left at the next corner, Jer," Herb reminded. "Remember now, wait till the leaders are even with the corner before you turn 'em. Keep the swing span and wheelers straight or even a little to the right. A little brake jus' before the corner lets the horses know you're gonna give 'em some directions."

Jeremiah nodded acknowledgment to the instructions and shifted his position, preparing for the turn. He glanced at the saloon on the corner and noticed a man, obviously drunk, clutching desperately to the pole that supported the porch overhanging the board-walk on which he stood.

Jeremiah pulled on the left reins, but to his chagrin not only the leaders but both the other spans also turned sharply left.

"One span at a time, Jer!" Herb cried.

The drunk on the corner looked wide-eyed at the team charging toward him, and he pushed away from the post and flattened himself against the saloon wall. Iron shoes smacked against the planks of the boardwalk as the wheelers tore past, and the stage rolled sharply to the right as the left front-wheel mounted the boardwalk and sheared off the post like a sickle felling a stalk of wheat. Herb threw himself to the right as the overhang slashed at the driver's seat and scraped angrily along the iron rail on the top of the stagecoach. The coach dropped to the ground for an instant and then bounded even higher as the left rear-wheel followed the path of the front. The stage dropped to the ground again, and Jeremiah desperately pulled the stage to a stop, this time hitting the brake on the first try.

His heart was pounding, and he glanced self-con-sciously at the people who gawked at him from the street and boardwalks. Reluctantly he looked at Herb and saw him with one hand on his stomach, another covering his eyes. Jeremiah feared the man was hurt.

"Herb?" Jeremiah asked tentatively. Then he realized that Herb was laughing—a sidesplitting, lung-busting laugh.

Herb stopped laughing long enough to gasp out a few words. "That's the God damned funniest thing I've ever seen, Jer. Did you see the look on his face?"

Jeremiah failed to see any humor in the incident and felt like shrinking down inside the boot and hid-ing.

The saloon owner came rushing out, and his mouth dropped when he saw the corner of his porch sagging and the post lying in the street. He stared at the stage, speechless.

"I'll take care of this," Herb said, and once again he climbed down from the box. Jeremiah watched him do some fast talking with the angry man and was surprised when Herb quickly bounded back onto the driver's seat. "All set," Herb said. Jeremiah wondered what he'd promised the man to clear things up so quickly, but he wasn't about to ask. He fumbled with the reins.

"Herb, I think you better drive."

"Nonsense," Herb said, "you're doin' fine, jus' fine. Let those horses go, Jer," he urged. "Let's see what we hit this time." He laughed.

Jeremiah gave him a pained look, but Herb just smiled broadly. With a deep breath, Jeremiah sent the horses off again at a fast pace, and the street in front of him cleared instantly. He managed to get the stage out of Lander without further mishap, and once on the gently curving road he actually relaxed a bit.

Concentrating so intently on driving the team, Jeremiah no longer had time to watch the scenery go by. He became even more impressed with Herb, for he could not understand how the man could drive the team and still spend so much time talking and gazing about. Herb tried to allay his tenseness by acting relaxed and unconcerned.

When the stage pulled into the Litle Popo Agie station, Jeremiah felt a great sense of relief; finally he could let go of the reins and forget about the horses for a moment. As he walked across the yard to the ranch house for a drink of water, he flexed the muscles of his hands. He couldn't remember them ever being so stiff before. But he was pleased with his accomplishment, and when the stage left, he handled the reins with a new, albeit fragile, confidence.

The stage now backtracked over the road it had traveled in the morning, out of the fertile Little Popo Agie valley, along the river and the red cliffs, up the forest-lined hill road, over the mountain saddle, and then down the other side into the dry Atlantic Gulch to Atlantic City. There they picked up a single additional letter, hardly worth the effort to stop the horses.

Shortly thereafter they reached South Pass City once again. Since there were no passengers aboard, Jeremiah drove the stage directly to the blacksmith shop and put the stage behind it, letting the horses into the corral. The mailpouch, express box, and freight articles were carried to the hotel lobby.

After a supper of leftovers, Herb took Jeremiah to the saloon, bought him a beer, and embarrassed him considerably by bragging about Jeremiah's prowess at the reins. But Jeremiah loved it.

He stayed for a while, played the piano a bit, and watched with growing interest the poker game that always started as long as there were at least two men in the saloon.

Watching the men play, and particularly Herb, he was struck by the thought that already he was developing a bond with the people of the area, a sense of belonging. A week earlier he would have sped past Point of Rocks in the train with no more than a casual glance at the small, grubby town. But now he knew the town, the people, how they laughed and how they cried, the history, the land.

He looked down at his hands and gingerly poked at the blisters that had formed. His hands were responding quickly to the evening's rest, for all those years of piano playing had strengthened them, but the reins had been hard on them. He rubbed his fingertips together. Would he lose his touch? Develop calluses, a tough skin that would obliterate any sensitivity to the feel of the ivory, destroy his sense of timing? Would he ever find his father's murderers and then proceed to San Francisco?

He contemplated his surroundings dejectedly. How different they were from what he had expected for himself at this time. Was this his destiny? He rubbed his hands over his weary face, then stretched the sore muscles of his shoulders and back. A good night's sleep would do wonders for his tired body and, hopefully, for his mental outlook.

CHAPTER TEN

Wednesday, June 22, 1880

Jeremiah's handling of the stage at departure was much better than the debacle in Lander, and he was relatively relaxed on the way south, actually conversing with Herb about topics other than stage driving. At each swing station he put the horses to a gallop and then brought the empty stage to a halt right in front of the doors of the buildings—more or less. He climbed down, grinning widely at the station personnel, proud of his achievement But Leon treated him as if he were a keg of salt pork. The Wilsons were more complimentary, but not effusive.

It was just after dark when he drove the stage down the main street of Point of Rocks, hoping people would note his presence at the reins. He stopped the stage in front of the Wells Fargo office with a loud "Whoa!"

From where he stood in the street, Seth reached out for the off leader. Anita came out of the office, her arms folded, a big smile evident even in the dim light from the office door.

"You made it," she called to Jeremiah.

"Yes, m'am," Jeremiah replied, wrapping the reins around the brake handle. "Herb says he'll make a first-rate jehu out of me yet."

"He's doin' fine, Anita," Herb confirmed. Anita stepped toward the door of the stage. "Cupboard's bare," Herb announced.

"Oh," Anita said disappointedly. Her arms fell to her sides.

"Note for you from Homer, though," he added, extending the envelope toward her. She took the letter.

Jeremiah climbed down to the ground and turned and took the express box from Herb, who then tossed the mailpouch on top of it. Herb sat down and unwound the reins.

"You can sleep here tonight, Herb," Anita suggested, realizing Herb wouldn't have time to return home for the night, since he had to drive the stage the next day again.

"No, thanks, Anita," he declined, somewhat awkwardly. "I'll find a soft spot over at the livery stable. I jus' couldn't sleep where your pa . . ."

Anita nodded. "I understand."

Seth jumped into the coach as Herb started it slowly, and they drove off for the livery stable.

Jeremiah carried the strong box and mailpouch into the office and set them down on the counter. He couldn't help but look down at the floor, and he noticed that, despite obvious vigorous scrubbing, dark stains remained on the wood planking.

Anita came in and went behind the counter. "No freight?" she asked.

Jeremiah broke out of his trance. He shook his head. "Only a couple of letters."

Anita sighed and peeked into the mailpouch. Then she opened the note from Homer. "There's going to be a gold shipment next Tuesday," she said, finishing reading.

"Oh," Jeremiah said. He thought of the information leaks in the past. "Why do they tell you ahead of time?"

"Well, we've sometimes put on extra guards," she explained. "Not that it did much good," she added poignantly.

"I see."

The young woman sorted the few letters that had arrived and then set the pouch on a shelf below the counter. She hoisted the empty strong box and put it on the floor.

"Well," Jeremiah said, "I guess I'll head over to the jail. I can sure use a good night's sleep."

"Oh," Anita spoke up. "How about you? You could stay here at the office if you like," she offered. "I know your mother would prefer your living here rather than in a jail cell."

"Here?"

"Yes, the back room is set up for housekeeping. My father stayed here often." She crooked a finger and picked up a lamp, and Jeremiah followed obediently. She led him to a small room just in back of the office proper. Its furnishings were Spartan but comfortable. A cot, small table, bowl and pitcher of water sitting on it, a potbellied stove, and a chair. "There's a small closet here," Anita said as she opened a narrow door and exposed some shirts and a coat. "My father's," she said reverently. "Haven't had the heart to get rid of them." She picked up the sleeve of the coat and pressed it to her cheek.

Jeremiah felt a lump forming in his throat. "What's this?" He reached in and picked up a rifle that was standing in a corner of the closet. It wasn't a Winchester. It was ponderous-looking with a large hammer and an involved metal mechanism over the breech.

"That was Father's, too," Anita said. "He brought it with him from the army. It's a Springfield carbine. His trapdoor carbine he called it."

"Trapdoor?" he asked.

"Yes. Here, I'll show you." She took the gun from his hands and stepped back into the center of the room, setting the lamp down on the table.

"You know how to use that?" he asked, surprised.

"This isn't Boston, Jeremiah," she chided. "First cock the hammer to the safety notch." She pulled back on the hammer with her thumb until it clicked.

"Then pivot the cam-latch lever and flip open the breechblock." She flipped the metal breechblock up, and a cartridge popped out of the breech and landed on the floor with a heavy clunk. "See the way it flipped open?"

"Just like a trapdoor," Jeremiah said, nodding.

Anita bent down and picked up the cartridge. "To reload just put the new cartridge in like this," she instructed as she inserted the cartridge into the breech, "and close the trapdoor." She smacked the breechblock down with the palm of her hand. "Pull the hammer back all the way and you're ready to fire." She pulled the hammer back until it clicked again, then pointed the carbine at the wall and sighted down the barrel.

"Careful," Jeremiah cautioned, apprehensive.

She laughed. "Silly," she said, smiling. She squeezed the trigger and let the hammer down gently with her thumb, then handed the weapon to Jeremiah. He put it back in the closet and closed the door.

He perused the spare room again. "Why did your father stay here when he had a nice home and you to come home to?" he asked.

Anita sighed. "I guess you'd find out eventually anyway," she said. "My father drank a lot. He always regretted leaving the army and then after Mother was killed he really started hitting the bottle hard. Couldn't face me at home for his shame, so he'd come here. I didn't want him to, but . . ."

"I'm sorry," Jeremiah said. "Had he been drinking the night he was killed?"

"I'm sure," she declared. "Otherwise the gang wouldn't have gotten the better of him. My father was a tough man," she said proudly.

"So the marshal told me," Jeremiah said, remembering the marshal's retort. Even in the dim light, Jeremiah could see that Anita's eyes were watering. "You must find it harder to be in here than Herb would," he observed softly.

"And you, too, I would suppose," she said sympathetically.

"Very."

She sniffled. "I find it hard to be in here, in the office, the town—"

"Are you thinking of leaving?"

She looked at him searchingly. "I don't really know anywhere else to go," she said. "I've given it some thought, even before Father was murdered."

Jeremiah nodded knowingly. "Herb told me about the plight of the stage line. The whole town for that matter."

Anita smiled weakly. "Did he make it sound like my whole world is crashing down on me?"

"Well . . ."

"He's right, I guess," she said, answering her own question. "Both parents murdered, Wells Fargo thinking of closing the office, no way to make a living here otherwise. Maybe I'd go to Rock Springs, or Green River, maybe even Cheyenne."

"Or farther?" he asked.

She looked at him intently, shifting her gaze from one of his eyes to the other. "How much farther?"

"Oh, I don't know," he said quickly, suddenly embarrassed. He wasn't sure why he'd asked that. Just a fleeting vision of the pretty young woman and himself walking down a street in San Francisco. He brushed the thought from his mind.

"I think I will stay here, Anita," he said, changing the subject.

"You don't have to if it—"

"No, I'll be all right. I'll have to get my gear from the jail." He paused. "Uh—could I see you home?"

Anita smiled at him. "I'd like that."

The two young people left the office, Anita locking the front door behind her and giving the key to Jeremiah. "I have another at home I can use," she said.

They walked down the boardwalk, Jeremiah's boots

clumping on the planks while Anita's small shoes tapped out a slow rhythm. They spoke not a word all the way to her house, both lost in their own reverie. She opened her front door and then turned to him.

"Thank you for accompanying me, Jeremiah," she said.

"My pleasure, Anita," he said and then fought for something more to say, not wanting her to leave. She started to enter the house. "Uh—I hope I do a good job driving the stage for you."

"I'm sure you will, Jeremiah," she said. "Herb's a good man; he'll teach you well." She glanced down at his hands. "Any blisters?" she asked, smiling.

He raised his hands and examined them. "Well, I guess they're not used to leather yet."

Anita took one of his hands in each of hers, and rubbed the blisters gently with her fingers. "They'll heal," she said, then paused. "Such strong hands," she commented, surprise in her voice. "All that piano playing, I guess."

Jeremiah nodded. "It keeps them well exercised." The gentle, soft touch of her fingertips on his hands gave him a delightful feeling of pleasure, and he was greatly disappointed when she stopped and let go.

"Anita," he said. "Uh—I know you're really my boss, I guess, but I'd be mighty pleased if—f—f you'd let me call on you." He trembled slightly.

Anita smiled and touched the dimple in his chin. "If you like," she said coyly.

Jeremiah nodded and smiled broadly. "Thank you, m'am," he said.

"Good night, Jeremiah," she said and then swished her way into the house.

"Good night, Anita," he said as the door closed. He raised his hands and stared at them a moment. Then he broke into whistling "Buffalo Gals" and skipped off the porch. He headed for the jail.

Just past the corner of the house a hand clamped

down on his shoulder and spun him around. A fist
smashed into his face, sending him flying backward
off his feet. He lay sprawled in the dust and, grimacing, put a hand to his cheekbone, where the skin had
been scraped off.

"I thought I made it clear, Bacon," Paul Warner
growled from where he stood towering over Jeremiah,
"that Anita is my woman." Jeremiah got slowly to
his knees. "That was just a warning," the deputy
said. "If I see you makin' eyes at her again, you
won't be able to get up even that far."

Two weeks ago Jeremiah would have tucked his tail
between his legs and skulked away, but this wasn't two
weeks ago. Rising abruptly, he lunged at his antag-
onist, ramming his head into the man's stomach and
knocking him hard against the side of the house.
Jeremiah was pleased at the sound of air rushing
from Paul's lungs and his head rapping against the
wood siding.

But Paul rallied immediately. He shook his head
once, then leaped at Jeremiah, pushing him backward. Jeremiah tried one swing, but Paul easily parried
his inept thrust. After that the deputy lashed out,
raining blows on Jeremiah's head and into his stomach,
short jabs and haymaker punches, each strike knocking Jeremiah backward.

Jeremiah sank to his knees and threw his arms
around the deputy's legs, but Paul kicked him away to
flop on his back on the ground, his heart pounding,
his lungs bursting, and blood flowing from his nose
and several cuts on his face.

Jabbing a finger painfully into Jeremiah's nose,
Paul stated his warning again. "She's mine," he
snarled. "Remember that." Then he straightened up,
adjusted his vest, and tucked his shirt in. He squared
his hat on his head and then strode off into the darkness.

Jeremiah lay on the ground trying to focus on the
stars overhead, wishing they would stop spinning

around so much. He rolled onto his side and reached for a handkerchief to stanch the flow of blood. Then he got to his feet and made his way painfully to the jail to pick up his belongings.

He was relieved to find that MacKenzie was absent from the office. He quickly gathered his belongings and left, heading unsteadily for the Wells Fargo office. He spent the night in its back room licking his wounds and hardening his resolve that Paul Warner would regret what he had just done.

CHAPTER ELEVEN

Thursday, June 23, 1880

The air was stale and still warm when Jeremiah walked into the Bitter Creek Saloon in the early evening; the coolness of the desert night had not yet reached the interior of the building. He went immediately to the far end of the bar where the food was set out. Nodding a greeting to Jason, who stood behind the bar wiping a glass as usual, he started to make himself a meat sandwich.

He put down a couple of pieces of cheese and then started to peel a hard-boiled egg while he ate the sandwich. Glancing about the saloon, he noted the sparse crowd—a few cowhands and townspeople. No wonder Zwieg wasn't interested in paying him on week-nights.

Stacey rose from a table and started walking in his direction, one hand on a hip, the other swishing the skirt of the same red dress she always wore. Jeremiah stopped chewing when he realized she was smiling, and he eyed her with suspicion.

"Evening, Jerry," she said sweetly, stopping in front of him.

He quickly swallowed the food in his mouth. "Evening, Stacey," he responded.

"You don't mind if I call you Jerry, do you? Jeremiah sounds so ancient."

"No, no," he reassured her. "Jerry will be fine."

"You going to play us some nice music tonight?"

"Thought I would, yes," he said.

"I saw you drive the stage in last night."

"Oh, did you?" he asked nonchalantly, but inwardly pleased that someone had noticed.

"That's a real tough job, driving a stagecoach."

He was flattered. "Oh, anybody could do it," he said with false modesty.

"Say, what happened to you?" she asked, concerned. She reached over to touch one of the abrasions on his face. "Oh, my."

"I fell," Jeremiah lied. "Stupid, wasn't it?"

"Looks to me like you were in a fight," she said, closing one eye and scrutinizing him.

"No, just a fall," he insisted.

Stacey smiled skeptically. "If you say so, Jerry." She reached over and took a piece of cheese and started nibbling on it. Jeremiah went back to eating his sandwich.

"You planning on being in Point of Rocks long, Jerry?"

"Well, I don't know," he replied. "I mean to stay here at least until the men who killed my father are caught."

"That could be a long time."

"And my mother may want to stay here because of Father," he added. "I'd want to stay and take care of her."

"Your mother?" Stacey laughed. "Oh, don't worry about her," she urged. "She's got herself a guardian angel—wearing a badge."

"What do you mean?" Jeremiah asked, suddenly displeased.

"Well, look, Jerry," Stacey said, as if she were stating the obvious. "Your mother's a good-lookin' woman yet. Anybody can see the marshal—"

"That's disgusting!" Jeremiah snapped. His mother and the marshal? That rough, uncouth man taking the place of his sophisticated and polished father? The thought of the lawman laying a hand on his mother revolted him. Actually he had never been able to envision his father passionately involved with his mother. Sex was for other people; parents were asexual. He knew that was silly, but he couldn't shake the thought.

"You fool," Stacey declared. "Why do you think everybody in town is fallin' all over themselves being so nice to you and your mother? A place to stay, jobs—"

"The town's just trying to be friendly," Jeremiah insisted.

"Hah! No town's that friendly. The marshal's twisted more arms than—"

"Stop it!"

Stacey changed suddenly. "Hey, I'm sorry, Jerry," she apologized. "Forget I said it, okay?"

Jeremiah gave her a stern look and was about to add something when Mel Zwieg came out of his office behind Jeremiah. He locked the office door and then came up to Jeremiah, slapping him on the back. "Evening, Jeremiah," he greeted.

"Evening, Mr. Zwieg," Jeremiah reciprocated.

"Was that you doing all the shooting this afternoon?"

"Yes, sir," Jeremiah confirmed. "And I'm getting a lot better."

"Think you'll ever get a chance to use your gun?"

"Never can tell," Jeremiah said, lifting his eyebrows. "There's a gold shipment coming in on the stage from Atlantic City the beginning of next week. If the Red Desert Gang makes a try for it, I'm hoping I'll get a chance to use my Colt." Suddenly he realized what he'd just revealed, and he quickly looked around to see who'd been listening. There seemed to be no one close enough to have overheard him clearly.

"Well, be careful," Zwieg warned.

"I'm not planning on taking any chances," Jeremiah declared.

"Good," the saloon owner said. He surveyed the nearly empty room, then turned to Stacey. "Dull night, huh?" he commented, then headed for the front door of the saloon.

"Sure as hell—sure is," Stacey called after him, catching herself in mid-phrase.

Jeremiah noted the correction with interest; Stacey had never shown the least reluctance to use profanity in the past.

"How long have you been in Point of Rocks, Stacey?"

"Couple o' years," she answered. "Though it seems like a couple o' centuries."

"How old are you?" he asked. "If you don't mind my asking," he added quickly.

"Twenty-two," she replied without hesitation.

Jeremiah looked surprised. He had thought she was at least thirty.

Stacey noticed the look. "Thought I was older, Jerry?" she asked.

"Well . . ."

"The life does it," she explained.

Jeremiah noted a tone of bitterness. "How did you become a—saloon girl?"

"Drunken father left home when I was just a tot, mother worked herself to death tryin' to support us all, the rest of the family scattered. Saloon work was all I could get. Pretty face, nice figure. I had no choice. I was fourteen on my first job."

"Fourteen!" Jeremiah felt compassion for Stacey.

"Now I'm trapped. No man would marry me, nobody would hire me for anything else. I'm trapped." She spoke softly, her voice trailing off.

Jeremiah stared at her. This was the real Stacey, he felt. The other, the profane, surly, boisterous, contemptuous woman he'd seen up to now was just a façade. She was really sensitive, tired, hurt, and lonely.

"I'm sorry, Stacey," he said gently.

She smiled at him. "Thanks." Then she laughed.

"But, hey," she said, "you got troubles of your own. You don't want to hear mine."

"No, that's all right. I—"

"How about playin' some music for me. Some real music." She pulled him by the arm. "Like they play in Boston."

"Well, okay," he said enthusiastically. They went to the piano. Jeremiah sat down, and Stacey leaned against the side of the instrument.

"Hey, Stacey!" a newly arrived cowboy shouted from the bar. Jeremiah turned to look at the man, who was walking toward them now. "How about a drink?" the man asked. "And some poker?"

"Sorry, cowboy," Stacey said. "I'm busy right now."

Jeremiah looked at her. Busy? That was her job. He was glad Zwieg had left.

"Poker and whiskey," the man repeated. He came up and grabbed Stacey by the arm.

Jeremiah rose to his feet instantly. "She said later," he snapped.

Stacey pulled away from the man's grasp and put her hands on Jeremiah's shoulders, pushing him back down. "Take it easy, Jerry," she said. "I can handle this." She turned to the cowboy again. "Get lost, mister," she said angrily.

The man looked Jeremiah up and down. "Better change his diapers," he said scornfully.

Jeremiah started to his feet again, but again Stacey restrained him. The man turned and walked back to the bar.

"It's part of my work, Jerry," she said. "Forget it. It doesn't bother me."

Jeremiah sat down and composed himself. "Poker," he said. "I'd like to learn that game someday. Herb seems to have a lot of fun at it."

"I could teach you," Stacey said eagerly. Jeremiah looked interested. "Hey, Jason, a deck of cards," she called to the bartender. A deck was quickly tossed to her. She sat Jeremiah at a table, opened the deck, and started to shuffle the cards.

"A little draw poker first," she suggested. "Each player gets five cards, looks at his hand, and then gets up to four new cards from the dealer in exchange for four he already has."

"I remember that," Jeremiah said. "But what are the various hands?"

"Oh, sorry," Stacey said. "Should have started with that. Lowest winning hand is simply the highest card."

"Okay, then what?"

"A pair, then two pair, three of a kind—"

"Hey, Stacey!" The cowboy was returning. "How come you play with him and not me?" he asked angrily.

Jeremiah jumped from his chair. Stacey leaped up, too. "Jerry, let's get away from him. He won't give us any peace." She grabbed the cards.

"What do you want with a calf like him when you could have a bull like— Hey!"

Stacey was pulling Jeremiah toward the stairs. Jeremiah followed reluctantly, glaring at the cowboy.

"Where are we going?" Jeremiah asked.

"My room."

He stopped short. "Your room?"

"Oh, come on," Stacey said, dragging him on. Jeremiah followed again, and she quickly had him to the top of the stairs. The cowboy stopped at the foot, grumbling and cursing. Stacey led Jeremiah to her room, ushered him in, and then closed the door.

It was a big room, untidy but pleasant. A large bed had the center of attention, but there was also a small, round table with a lighted kerosene lamp on it to one side of the room. There were also several chairs, a dressing table, curtains on the windows, pictures on the walls, and two small stands, one with a bowl and pitcher on it, the other piled with assorted articles.

Jeremiah gaped at a closet full of clothes that showed behind a folding screen.

"I don't waste those on cowhands," Stacey said, noting his stare.

"I always thougnt—"

"I can imagine. Tell you what," she suggested. "I'll wear something different, just for you." She handed him the cards and headed for the closet.

"No, that's all right," he said. "I like the red dress."

"It'll only take a minute," she said, pulling a garment off a hanger and stepping behind the screen. "Put the cards on the table."

Jeremiah did as he was directed, then looked back. The red dress arced over the screen and draped over it. He swallowed and looked around nervously.

"Stacey," he said. "I don't think I should be here like this."

"Don't be silly," she said. "I'm almost ready." There was a pause and then she stepped from behind the screen. She was dressed in a garment of almost gossamer fineness, her figure hidden in an explosion of frills and laces. She walked up to Jeremiah. "How does this look?"

Jeremiah stared at the cloth and could make out the tone of her skin beneath it. He looked up to her face, and she tossed her head, making her red-brown tresses tumble over her shoulders. Jeremiah's breathing accelerated; his heartbeat did likewise.

Stacey leaned over and blew out the flame in the lamp, plunging the room into the darkness. Jeremiah could hear her undoing a sash, and the soft rustle of the cloth made him suck in his breath.

"S-Stacey . . ."

She took his hands in hers, holding them palm forward. "Such nice hands," she said. "Strong, sensitive." She tucked them inside her garment and placed them gently on her bare breasts. "Ever play on a keyboard like that before, Jerry?" she asked softly. She reached up and kissed him on the lips.

"I—gotta go," Jeremiah said slowly.

"Stay," she appealed. "Stay and I'll make a man of you."

He stayed.

CHAPTER TWELVE

Friday, June 24, 1880

Jeremiah had heard his father open his watch hundreds of times, and he was sure that the cover that had just been opened at the table behind him that evening was that of his father's watch. He had just finished a tune when that tiny, almost inaudible *sproing!* had come like a clap of thunder.

Jeremiah turned quickly. A cowboy was looking at the face of a watch he held in his hand not eight feet away from Jeremiah's eyes, which were filled with loathing. He got up as the man snapped the cover shut and dropped the watch into his pocket. Jeremiah walked up carefully behind the man and with a quick thrust removed the fellow's Colt from its holster.

"Hey!" the man barked, scowling up at Jeremiah.

Jeremiah cocked the hammer of the pistol and then shoved the barrel up against the cowboy's nose. The man dropped the cards he'd just picked up, his mouth dropped open, and his eyes crossed as they focused on the gun barrel. All activity in the saloon stopped, and a hush fell over the crowd.

"Let's see the watch," Jeremiah demanded.

The cowboy licked his lips, then reached into his pocket and pulled the watch out, never taking his eyes off the pistol.

"Hand it to the fellow on your left," Jeremiah ordered. The man complied.

"Okay, mister," Jeremiah said to the man who now held the watch, "turn the watch over There should be a date there: June second, eighteen fifty-eight."

"That's the date all right," the examiner confirmed.

Jeremiah jammed the pistol barrel harder against the man's nose. "That was my father's watch," he declared, "and it was taken off his body by the man who killed him."

"Killed!" the cowboy exclaimed fearfully. "I didn't kill nobody," he pleaded. "I bought that watch from a cowhand. I swear!"

"Liar!" Jeremiah yelled.

"He's right, mister," another of the card players spoke up. Jeremiah shifted his glare to the new speaker. "I seen him buy it, jus' like he says," the man affirmed.

Another man approached the other side of the table. "When was your pa killed, piano player?" the man asked.

"A week ago Wednesday," Jeremiah informed him.

"A week ago Wednesday?" his victim echoed. "Hell, boss, we were over a hundred miles south of here then," he said to the man standing across from Jeremiah.

"That's right," the trail boss said. "We just delivered a herd of Texas breeders to the Circle G yesterday. We were nowheres near here when your pa was killed."

Jeremiah was suddenly filled with doubt.

"There's two dozen men that says Wilkie there couldn't've killed your pa," the man continued. A general murmur indicated agreement. "If you're lookin' for the killer, I suggest you go after the fellow who sold Wilkie the watch."

Jeremiah considered for a moment. He had no reason not to believe the two dozen men. He pulled the gun away and let the hammer down, at which Wilkie let out a great sigh of relief. Jeremiah handed him his gun. "I'm sorry," he apologized. "I've got the wrong man."

The cowboy nodded and rubbed his nose, then holstered his gun.

"What was the name of the man who sold you the watch?" Jeremiah asked.

"Gordie. Gordie somethin', I forget the last name."

"Gordie Hodson," Jeremiah repeated, surprised to find it was his old nemesis. MacKenzie hadn't been able to come up with anything when he'd gone to see him.

"Yeah, that was the name," the man said. "Sold it to me for ten dollars."

"You got a bargain," Jeremiah said. "I'll give you more than ten dollars for the watch. I'd like to have it back to give to my mother."

Wilkie took the watch from his poker partner and handed it to Jeremiah. "Take it for free, piano player, I don't want nothin' with blood on it. Tell your ma I'm sorry for her."

Jeremiah stared at the familiar watch in his hand and felt a renewed pang of grief. "Thank you," he said. "And I'm sorry about the gun." He started to back away from the table. He turned to Jason at the bar "Jason, a beer and a whiskey for the cowboy—on me."

Jason nodded, and Jeremiah retreated farther from the table. He stuck the watch in his pocket, turned, and walked briskly out the door. Action resumed inside the saloon.

Jeremiah was soon in the back room of the Wells Fargo office. He went directly to the closet, opened the door, and pulled out his gunbelt. He slapped it on, then grabbed Kessler's Springfield carbine along with a box of cartridges, which he stuck in his vest pocket. Hurriedly he left the office and headed for the livery stable.

The big doors in front were locked from the inside, but a small door to the side was open. Jeremiah entered and closed the door quietly behind him. It was nearly pitch-black inside the stable except for a narrow shaft of moonlight coming in from a small window high in the back wall. A man's snoring could be heard coming from a small room across from Jeremiah, and he walked slowly in that direction, feeling his way with his feet.

Inside the small room the smell of straw, hay, and manure was mixed with the new odor of sweat, urine, and alcohol. Jeremiah could make out a form on a cot. He stepped toward it, and his foot kicked a bottle that bounced off the wooden leg of the cot with a hollow clink. Jeremiah leaned over the sleeping figure and tapped him on the shoulder.

"Seth," he said. There was no response. "Seth," he repeated, louder. He shook Seth's shoulder. "Hey, wake up, you drunk," he almost shouted. The snoring stopped with a gasp.

'Wha—" Seth's hand moved erratically for the wall to steady himself.

'Seth," Jeremiah said. "It's me, Jeremiah Bacon. Wake up."

'Jeremiah?"

'Yes. I need a horse. Can you get me a horse?"

'Wha' ya wanna horse for?" the man asked, irritated. "Wha' time is it?"

"I need a horse, Seth," Jeremiah repeated once more. "I need it real bad."

"Well, take one," Seth said impatiently. "Leave a dollar on the barrel," he added, rolling over again.

"No, Seth, wait," Jeremiah said, rolling him back again. "I don't know which one."

"Take the dun," Seth suggested. He tried to break away.

"Seth, I don't know which one is a dun." He pulled hard on the man. "Show me." Seth only mumbled. Jeremiah nearly pulled him off the cot. "I need a horse, Seth. You got to saddle it for me. I don't know how."

'You gotta be kiddin'," Seth said, incredulous.

'Come on, Seth," Jeremiah pleaded. "I'll buy you a bottle, too."

"Oh, all right," the livery man said. He pushed Jeremiah's helping hand away and staggered to his feet. Seth fumbled for something on a table, and then a match burst into flame. Jeremiah squinted at the sudden light. He was aghast to watch the drunken man swaying about with a lighted match in his hand in the middle of the highly flammable stable.

Seth managed, however, to light a lantern, adjust the wick, and blow out the match without setting the place afire. He picked up the lantern and headed for the stable area, there hanging the lantern on a peg protruding from one of the main posts. He went into a stall and came out leading a horse with a halter.

"You watch," Seth said, "so next time you wanna go gallavantin' 'round in the middle o' the night, you can do it for yourself." He took off the halter and looped it around the horse's neck, then selected a bridle from several that lay in a pile. He put the bit into the horse's mouth and slipped the split-ear crown-piece over the horse's ears. "Gimme that blanket," he said, lifting the halter free.

Jeremiah pulled a blanket off the stall wall and handed it to Seth. The latter expertly flipped it onto the horse's back and smoothed it out. Then he went to the other side of the stable and hoisted a saddle off a rail. He carried it back to the horse and tossed it onto the blanket, adjusting it slightly. Then he hooked the stirrup over the saddle horn, reached under the horse's belly and grabbed the cinch from the other side. He fastened a leather strap to the rigging ring and pulled the cinch tight. The stirrup was let down and the reins were placed over the horse's head.

"His name's Bobby," Seth said. "Good little gelding," he added, patting the horse's neck. The animal whickered softly. "That's one dollar—in advance."

Jeremiah reached into his pocket and pulled out a dollar, which he dropped into Seth's outstretched hand. Seth headed for the big doors to open them, and Jeremiah picked up the carbine and started to mount the horse from the right side.

"Hey," Seth called. "Other side."

"Why?"

"Hell, I don't know. Always mount on the left."

Jeremiah went to the other side and swung clumsily into the saddle. "Okay, Bobby, let's go," he urged.

"You ever ride before?" Seth asked suspiciously.

"No," Jeremiah answered.

"Oh, God," Seth groaned. "Well, give 'im a kick to go. Lay the reins on his neck to turn 'im. Left side to go right and t'other way around."

"Okay." Jeremiah gave Bobby a slight kick, and the horse walked out of the stable. Jeremiah reined him in.

"Hey, Seth," he said. "How do I get to the Circle G?"

Seth walked up to the horse and rider and looked up at Jeremiah. "You ain't thinkin' o' ridin' out there now, are you?"

"Just give me the directions, Seth. Don't play mother hen."

"There's no roads out there," Seth cautioned. "Just desert, hills, grass, sage—"

"Seth!" Jeremiah said impatiently.

Seth shrugged. "Follow the tracks west 'bout four miles, then south to the creek, cross it, keep on ten, twelve miles, then east aways. Ranch's in a little valley that runs east and west. Some red cliffs behind it, and another creek runs through it."

"Thanks," Jeremiah said, and he gave Bobby another jab with his heels.

"You'll never find it," Seth called after the young man.

CHAPTER THIRTEEN

Saturday, June 25, 1880

Jeremiah pulled the gelding to a stop at the stream's edge, and the horse lowered his head and drank lustily from the brown fluid that crept past its hooves. The hot, sweating young man squinted at the late afternoon sun that beat down unmercifully, as it had done all day. He gazed at the red sandstone bluffs that rose from the other side of the stream. Did all streams in this country look the same? Or was this the same stream he'd crossed several times before?

Since Jeremiah had left Point of Rocks the previous night he hadn't seen a house, a campfire, or cowboy, or more than two or three steers. The hills seemed identical, one hill looked like the next or the last, one gully and valley like another. A monotonous parade of creeks, buttes, sagebrush, greasewood, and grass. He could be two miles from Point of Rocks or a hundred.

Jeremiah climbed wearily from the saddle, hanging on to the saddle horn as he slowly let his feet and legs adjust to standing on firm ground again. He hadn't realized how uncomfortable and actually painful sitting in a saddle all day could be. His muscles ached, and his skin was chafed. The compulsion to touch his knees together had become unbearable, and yet, when he dismounted, his legs were so stiff that it hurt when he tried to do just that.

He stepped away from Bobby, and the horse took several steps farther into the water. Jeremiah laid the Springfield carbine on the ground, and the gunbelt and pistol, which seemed to weigh a ton by now, were soon lying on top of the carbine.

Jeremiah walked unsteadily to the stream and knelt down in the moist sand. He took off his hat and dropped it aside, then scooped up the water and splashed it onto his face. Warm as it was, the liquid felt refreshing as it washed away a day's accumulation of sweat and dirt. He stuck his head into the water.

A bullet smacked into the water a foot in front of Jeremiah's face. Jeremiah choked on some water and leaped back whirling toward the sound of the gunshot.

"Make yourself comfortable, piano player," Gordie Hodson said from the top of a small hill to Jeremiah's right, a revolver in his hand.

Jeremiah shot a glance at his own weapons lying in pile behind himself, so close, yet so far away. He felt sick, and a surge of fear made his skin turn hot and his body tremble. His heart began to pump furiously.

Gordie walked slowly down the hill. "For a greenhorn," he said, "you're one hell of a tracker. You must be part Indian or coyote or somethin'."

Jeremiah couldn't help releasing a nervous, ironic chortle.

"What's so funny?" Gordie snapped.

"I—I wasn't following you," Jeremiah stammered. "I was lost."

"Lost!" The other man roared with laughter. "You mean you found me by accident?" He laughed again. "Well, that's too bad, kid," he said finally. "But I'm glad it was you who came along; I was expectin' the marshal."

Jeremiah wondered why Gordie had been expecting the marshal, but he didn't dwell on the puzzle.

"I'd have been a lot farther away by now," Gordie said, "if my horse hadn't gone lame. Kind of you to bring me another. Sorry I'll have to repay the favor by killin' you, but I can't take the chance of someone findin you alive. MacKenzie must be out here 'somewhere lookin' for me. Damn that Texan!"

The Texan with the watch! Somehow Gordie had found out about the confrontation in the saloon and assumed that Jeremiah would have told Otis about it.

"You going to shoot me down just like you did my father?"

"Like father, like son," Gordie said. He laughed.

Jeremiah glared at him, still on his knees, his trembling fingers digging into the sand in rage and frustration. But, as afraid of dying as he was, he wasn't going to beg or grovel at the feet of his father's murderer. Even more than dying, he regretted with seething anger that his oath of vengeance could not be carried out.

"Well, Bacon," the outlaw said, "can't waste time jabberin'; gotta put distance between me and the marshal. Sorry 'bout this. You played the piano real good." He raised the pistol a trifle to aim it squarely at Jeremiah's chest.

Gordie's hat flew off as if an unseen hand had batted it off his head. "The hell?" Gordie blurted, startled, and then both men heard the sound of a rifle shot. Gordie looked up past Jeremiah, quickly raised his pistol and fired off a shot. Jeremiah turned around in time to see Otis MacKenzie lever another cartridge into the chamber of his Winchester and take aim again.

Gordie spun aside, and the second rifle bullet also missed, kicking up a spout of sand behind him. But his desperate maneuver threw him off balance in the loose sand, and he fell on his side, hitting his elbow. The pistol popped from his grasp and landed in the stream with a pathetic *ploop!* He stared bug-eyed at the small ripples in the brown water, then looked quickly at Jeremiah.

The same thought struck both men; they both dove

for Jeremiah's weapons, landing on the guns simul-
taneously. They grappled in the sand, clawing and
swinging furiously.

Otis cursed from where he knelt on the rimrock. He
cursed himself for having missed what should have
been a shot of only moderate difficulty, and he cursed
Jeremiah for forcing him to try to kill a man he
wanted very badly to take alive. And now with the
pair rolling in the sand he couldn't get off another
shot. And yet, with the two men struggling as they
were, there was a chance he could still grab Hodson
without killing him.

Otis ran for his horse, mounted, darted looks both
ways for the fastest route down to the stream, then
galloped the horse off to the right.

At the stream's edge, Gordie was putting his big-
ger size to good advantage. Jeremiah's face was trailing blood from his nose and his lip; his ribs throbbed
with pain from Gordie's fierce blows.

The two men rolled into the stream, Jeremiah landing first, just at the edge of the water. The momentum
of the struggle, however, carried Gordie right on
over, and the outlaw found himself on his back with
his face submerged. He released his hold on Jeremiah
and frantically thrashed about, trying to get his face
above water and break away from Jeremiah's grasp.
He flailed wildly at Jeremiah and desperately clawed
his face.

Jeremiah tried to throw punches, but the water
blunted his blows. So he reached down and clamped
both hands tightly on the outlaw's throat. Gordie
grabbed his wrists and tried to pull them off, but to no
avail. He bucked and reared like a horse being broken,
swung at Jeremiah blindly, and tore at his hands.
Jeremiah thought of his father lying in a pool of
blood. He thought of his mother sobbing over his
body and singing at the grave. He squeezed tighter.

A large series of bubbles broached the surface. Gordie's spasmodic movements decreased in intensity, and finally the struggling stopped altogether.

When MacKenzie's horse splashed into the stream behind him, Jeremiah's hands were still locked firmly in their hold. "Don't drown him, Bacon!" Otis shouted. The marshal leaped from the still-moving horse and pounced on Jeremiah. "Don't kill him!" He violently yanked the startled Jeremiah off the outlaw. Otis reached down and grabbed Gordie and dragged him toward the shore, with Jeremiah watching dumbfounded from where he sat in the water.

Otis laid the body on the sand and felt for signs of life. Then he stood up. "God damn you!" he shouted at Jeremiah. "You killed him!"

Jeremiah was indignant and perplexed at the marshal's rage. "He killed my father," he sputtered in retort. It was both accusation and justification.

"I know that," Otis snarled impatiently. "But Hodson wasn't the only one in on that murder. Alive, he could've given us the best lead on the gang I've ever had, and God dammit, you fouled it up." Otis took off his hat and threw it on the ground.

Jeremiah was struck by the logic of the man's statement. "Damn," he said to himself. He looked at the marshal. "He would have killed me," he apologized, deflated.

"Didn't you hear me calling?" the marshal asked angrily. "I would've been here like that," he said, snapping his fingers. "God damn you," he repeated. He turned and stalked off a few paces, then turned and came back to the stream's edge to glare at Jeremiah. The young man stood up slowly. Water dripped from his clothes; blood covered his face and torn shirt. He was extensively cut and bruised. Otis looked down at the dead man. It could have been Jeremiah, he thought.

"Well," he said in a softer tone, "at least we got one

of the bastards." He looked at Jeremiah again. "You hurt bad?"

Jeremiah shook his head stubbornly. "I'll live," he said. He sloshed his way out of the water and stood over the still form lying on the sand. One down, three to go, he thought.

Otis was tying his horse to a small stump nearby where a few tufts of sickly grass struggled for survival. Jeremiah walked up to him. "How'd you find me?" he asked.

"I didn't," Otis informed him. "I was following Gordie."

Jeremiah's gratitude faded a bit. "I was lost, you know," he said, disgruntled to realize that the marshal's concern for him was only incidental to his finding the outlaw.

"I know," Otis said matter of factly. He fumbled in his saddlebags and brought out a bandanna and handed it to Jeremiah. "Clean yourself up a bit," he suggested.

Jeremiah dabbed at the bleeding cuts on his face. "How'd you know about Gordie?"

"Seth woke me about dawn," Otis said. "Told me he was worried about your havin' ridden off into the desert in the dead of night. Actually," he interjected with a smile, "I think he was worried about gettin' his horse back."

Jeremiah saw no humor in it. "Seth didn't know about Gordie."

"No, but Zwieg did. Seth told me you asked about directions to the Circle G, so I figured I'd better hightail it out to the ranch to prevent you from gettin' killed. But Earl Gilham hadn't seen you by the time I got to the Circle G, so I knew you were lost. And Earl also told me somebody had come by to see Gordie Hodson earlier. The rider called Gordie outside, talked to him for a minute, then rode off. Gordie packed his gear and rode off, hell bent for leather right after that."

"How come you chose to go after Gordie rather than find me?" Jeremiah asked, a bit peeved.

"A day's lead would've gotten Gordie clear out of the territory," Otis said. "I knew I'd find you wanderin' in a circle somewhere." Otis pulled a leather pouch out of a saddlebag. "You bring any food with you?"

"No."

"Any water?"

Jeremiah shook his head, embarrassed.

"You're a fool, Bacon," Otis said.

"I learned my lesson," Jeremiah confessed, remembering the terrifying feeling of being lost, the burning thirst, the fear of death.

"And," Otis said critically, "if I hadn't heard a shot and come over to the rim to investigate, you'd be lying on that sand instead of Gordie."

Jeremiah shuddered involuntarily.

"Catching those murderers is my job, Bacon," Otis said firmly "You stay out of it He waved a hand toward Gordie s body. "Look how you messed things up "

"You'd have killed him anyway," Jeremiah said in defense.

"No, I wouldn't've, Otis argued. "If you hadn't been around I'd've winged him, disabled him. Taken him back to Point of Rocks where we could've gotten some information out of him He paused. "Then we'd've hung him."

"I've got to do it myself, Marshal," Jeremiah said. "It's just something I have to do."

"No, it's not!" Otis said angrily. "You'll only get yourself killed and give your mother more grief. But most important—you're gettin' in my way, Bacon." Otis pointed a finger at Jeremiah. "Now, listen good. You get any other leads about any member of the Red Desert Gang you tell me and let me handle it from there. Don't interfere!" He emphasized his order by jabbing his finger into Jeremiah's chest.

Jeremiah swallowed and nodded. "Yes, sir," he said.

"Okay," the marshal said, relaxing. He held the pouch out to Jeremiah. "Have some cheese and dried beef," he offered.

"Thanks," Jeremiah said gratefully and dug into the pouch greedily. He tore off a chunk of the meat and chewed the tough fibers slowly, savoring the flavor. He popped a bit of cheese into his mouth, too. "Where are we, anyway?"

"Salt Wells Creek. 'Bout forty miles south o' town."

Jeremiah paused in his chewing. He had missed the ranch by thirty miles.

"Gordie's horse is lame," Otis said. "We'll use yours to carry the body and ride double on mine." The marshal handed Jeremiah another piece of meat, took one for himself, then closed the pouch and stuffed it back into the saddlebag.

"Help me get Gordie's body on your horse," Otis said as he started toward where the outlaw lay. Jeremiah obeyed, retrieving Bobby from where he'd wandered. Otis stood at Gordie's head, and Jeremiah went to his feet. He reached for the man's knees but stopped. He stared at his hands. Otis looked up at him, puzzled.

"Somethin' wrong?" he asked.

"Well," Jeremiah said hesitantly. "It's funny. I wanted this man dead in the worst way. I wanted to kill him myself. I thought I would be pleased and gratified. But having done it, I'm neither."

"Well," Otis said, standing up and putting his fists on his hips. "Maybe there's some hope for you yet, Bacon. Killin' is a mean, dirty job, no matter what the reason. But don't go frettin' about sendin' this one to his Maker. We all die sooner or later, and it's better for the rest of us if his kind die sooner rather than later

"You've killed men, haven't you, Marshal?"

"Yes, but I never liked it. It was a job that had to be done. There's somethin' wrong with a man who enjoys killin'. I've seen thousands of men killed—"

"Thousands?"

"In the war. Iron Brigade, from Michigan—"

"Michigan?" Jeremiah asked, astonished. "You're from Michigan?"

Otis nodded.

"Gee, I always thought you were born out here. You seem part of this country."

"No, came out here to forget the war, if I could. I was doin' a job I thought needed doin', but I didn't like it. Thousands of men killin' other thousands of men, and all of them feelin' the same as I did, I suspect, no matter which side they were on."

"Then you came out here to Point of Rocks?"

"Indirectly," Otis said. He took his hat and wiped the perspiration from his brow. "All I knew before the war was farmin', but you can't farm out here. All I learned in the war was killin', so I drifted into law work. One town led to another 'til I wound up here." He took a look around. "But the country grows on you. You'll see."

"How come you never married?"

Otis stared at the young man. "Awful nosy, aren't you, Bacon?"

"Sorry."

Otis felt a compulsion to talk anyway, despite his usual reticence. Standing over another man's body turned him introspective. Life and death, where he was, where he'd been, where he was going.

"Never found a woman I wanted or that wanted me even if I wanted her," he went on. "And desirable women are scarce out here."

"How about saloon girls?" Jeremiah asked. "Do they make good wives?"

Otis eyed Jeremiah suspiciously. A smile appeared, and he closed one eye. "You aren't thinkin' o' marryin' Stacey just because she's had you to bed once, are you?"

"Stacey? She—we—nothing like that," Jeremiah

blustered, but he felt a glow rise on his face, and his ears twitched backward.

"No, 'course not," Otis said, chuckling. He pondered a moment. "I suppose they can make good wives. Maybe it depends on whether they marry good husbands. I don't know. I guess it's a risk some men are willin' to take, in view of the supply situation. That's why someone like your mother, a fine, decent, good-lookin' woman is a veritable treasure out here. She can have—" He stopped. He wiped his hands on his pants nervously. "Sorry, Bacon," he apologized. "I spoke out o' line sayin' somethin' like that with your father just . . ." Otis took a deep breath and stared vacantly past Jeremiah at the bluffs in the distance.

Jeremiah stared at the marshal, surprised by the streak of sensitivity, even compassion, which he had not noticed before. He looked down at his own hands. What marvelous instruments hands were. Strong, supple, capable of infinitely diverse movements, of delicate touches—or violent action. How sensitive the fingertips were! Texture, warmth, hardness, pain. The smooth gloss of the ivory keys of a piano, the sweaty pliability of the leather reins of a stage team, the soft firmness of a woman's breast—or the wet roughness of a drowning man's throat.

Left hand, right hand. Life, death. Stacey, Anita. The piano, the desert. Kill or be killed.

"Lend a hand, Bacon," Otis said, reaching down. "We got a long ride ahead of us, and we'll have to take it slow with two on one horse."

CHAPTER FOURTEEN

Sunday, June 26, 1880

"No, you keep the watch, Jeremiah," Priscilla Bacon said to her son. "I think your father would be proud to have you carry it."

Jeremiah gulped down a growing lump in his throat. "Thank you, Mother," he said softly. His fingers ran over the filigreed cover of his father's watch, and then he put it into his own pocket. He smiled tenderly at his mother, and she reciprocated.

"Supper's on," Anita called from the dining room. The two people turned toward the dining room and the pleasant aroma of hot roast beef and potatoes.

"We're coming, Anita," Priscilla said. "Anita's an excellent cook, Jeremiah," she added as an aside.

Jeremiah helped his mother with her chair and repeated the courtesy for Anita, who smiled appreciatively. The meal was superb, and Jeremiah ate greedily, having had nothing more than the dried beef and cheese the marshal had brought along on the ride and later some beans in his office after they had deposited Gordie s body at Pierce's store. Jeremiah had then gone to the Wells Fargo office for a long sleep.

"Jeremiah," his mother said as the three started in on the apple pie dessert, "I wasn't going to tell you about this until I had some definite news on the subject, but I have written to Professor Peters at the university, asking him to find some way for you to continue your studies."

"My studies?" Jeremiah asked, somewhat surprised. "But, Mother, I can't leave Point of Rocks."

"I will miss you, Jeremiah, if I stay here," she said. "However, I may accompany you to San Francisco. In any eventuality, it is obvious that if you stay here, your talent for the piano will be wasted."

"I can't leave you, Mother," Jeremiah insisted. "I'd be shirking my duty and responsibility—to you and to Father."

"Son," Priscilla said, "I suspect that your strong desire to stay here is not entirely due to concern for me. It is more a sense of mission that keeps you here, an unholy drive for vengeance."

"Mother, I—"

"Jeremiah, I hardly know you anymore," she said sadly. "What has happened to the piano? Now, you've slept in a jail, you frequent a saloon, you've taken to drinking beer, and now the ultimate—you've killed a fellow human being. With your bare hands, no less."

"Mother, he was one of Father's—"

"Look at your hands, Jeremiah," she ordered.

Obediently he glanced down at the hand holding his fork with a large slice of apple skewered on it.

"Those hands were meant for great things, Jeremiah," she declared. "Things noble, honorable, in the highest tradition of music."

"Mother—"

"And now you produce works base, unworthy."

Jeremiah flinched. He couldn't remember ever seeing such fire in his mother's eyes.

"Can't you see that this quest for revenge has clouded your judgment?" Priscilla pleaded. "Can't you see that you must leave?"

Jeremiah stared at his apple pie, torn between a desire to reassure his mother and an even stronger conviction that he wouldn't leave until all four of his father's murderers were dead.

"We should hear from Professor Peters shortly,"

Priscilla said. "I pray every night and morning that it will be favorable, Jeremiah."

"Mother . . ." He saw that it was futile to argue. He looked at Anita, but the young woman only stared down at the steam rising slowly from the surface of the coffee in her cup. Jeremiah finished his pie silently.

The rest of his stay that afternoon was filled with embarrassing pauses and strained conversation. After an hour he felt he'd stayed long enough to be polite and took his leave. Anita saw him to the door and stepped out into the front yard with him.

"You going to practice shooting this afternoon, Jeremiah?" she asked, subdued.

"Yes," he answered. He looked down into Anita's dark eyes. "Do you think I'm doing wrong, Anita?" he asked.

"I don't know, Jeremiah," she said. "I fully understand your feelings, your desire to see your father avenged." She sighed. "On the other hand, maybe my judgment's clouded, too. After all, if you catch your father's murderers you also catch my father's murderers—and my mother's."

"Oh."

"I can see two dangers in your plans, Jeremiah," she stated.

"Two?"

"Yes," she said. "One is that you may get killed. These men are tough, seasoned outlaws; they've had years of experience out here."

"I know what you mean," Jeremiah said, remembering looking down the bore of Gordie's forty-five. "But that's why I practice all I can."

"Secondly, there's a fine line between seeing justice done and seeing justice done in. When do you cross the line from one side of the law to the other? When are you the righteous avenger and when the cold-blooded murderer yourself?"

Jeremiah didn't answer but gazed intently into those fascinating brown eyes of hers. Strangely, he found her arguments much more persuasive than those of his mother.

"Jeremiah," she said earnestly, reaching for his arm with her hands. "I'd hate to see you killed. I'd hate to see your mother suffer more. I'd hate to see her grieving because you'd been killed, too. And think what it would do to her, if you were hanged for taking the law into your own hands."

Jeremiah's scalp cringed. His *own* hanging had never crossed his mind.

"If that school thing comes through, Jeremiah," Anita urged, "take it. Leave Point of Rocks. Become the great pianist your mother says you can become."

Jeremiah was deeply touched by the woman's expression of concern, both for himself and for his mother. He hated to see the frown on Anita's pretty face. He smiled. "Mother is somewhat prejudiced," he said. "I'm not sure I can become great. Excellent, certainly, but great?"

Anita frowned. "Your mother says you have a rare talent for the piano." -

"Uncommon, yes," he said. "Rare?" He shrugged his shoulders.

"Jeremiah," Anita asked, "are you seriously thinking of not leaving—ever?"

"It's getting harder to leave all the time, Anita," he said. "At first it was just my mother and those four men. Now . . ." He shook his head as if to clear it. "I don't know. I've been confused lately. My whole life up 'til now has been music, mostly the piano. I keep trying to think if that was a conscious decision or not. It's always been there, like eating lunch or going to bed at night. But in the short time I've been out here I've met a whole new world. There's a vitality, an intensity to life out here that I've never known before. I keep telling myself that it's just the shock of my father's death, but I'm confused. I don't know."

Jeremiah looked at Anita and said softly, "There's another factor, too." He placed a hand on hers where it still rested on his arm.

Anita blushed and bowed her head. Jeremiah felt excited.

"Well," she said as she gave his arm a slight squeeze. "I'd better get back to your mother. Good afternoon, Jeremiah," she said, smiling brightly.

"Good afternoon, Anita," Jeremiah returned, and he beamed as she ever so slowly withdrew her hand from his.

"Osborne," Otis MacKenzie called.

"Oh, hello, Marshal," the banker said, turning on the boardwalk. "Hear you and Bacon got one of the Red Desert Gang. Good work."

"Yeah," the lawman said, walking up to Osborne. "Thanks." He stopped and rubbed his chin. "Say, Frank, uh . . ."

"Yes?"

"That Orville place, on Vermilion Creek?"

"Yes?"

"That still for sale?"

The banker was taken aback. "*You* want to buy it?" He laughed.

"Can't be a lawman forever," the marshal explained. "Just curious, that's all."

"Yeah, sure, Otis," the banker said. "It's still for sale. I could probably get you a good price on it, too. Orville's brother in Cheyenne is anxious to clear up the estate; it's been hanging in the air for a long time. It's not the best ranch in the area, you know," he cautioned.

"I know. I took another look at it last week. But then I don't have that much money," Otis pointed out.

"Well—" The banker knew what Point of Rocks paid its marshal. "Want me to get an asking price for you?"

"Yeah," the marshal said. "Just curious, though," he added quickly.

"Sure, just curious," Osborne repeated.

"See you around, Frank," Otis said and started back the way he'd come.

"Yes, 'bye, Otis." The banker smiled to himself. He could smell a sale a mile off.

It was getting hard to see the tin cans in the twilight, but Jeremiah kept practicing. He had improved immensely. Given six cans, he could draw and hit perhaps half of them, though his speed was still well below that of the marshal's. Nevertheless, he was probably already better than most of the men in the area, which was not surprising since he'd probably shot off more cartridges in a week than most men did in their lifetimes.

"You're gettin' better," a voice said behind him. Jeremiah whirled, startled at the sound. Paul Warner faced him.

"Thanks," Jeremiah said. He continued to load his forty-four.

"Maybe catch up to the marshal someday," the deputy surmised.

"I'll never be that good," Jeremiah said. "But maybe I don't have to be."

"Mm," Paul considered. "Otis told me the way you did in that Gordie fellow. You've got good hands. Just shows you hands can be more important than a gun sometimes," Paul said.

"Guess you're right," Jeremiah agreed.

"I can think of other situations where you might not get a chance to use your gun," the deputy suggested.

"For instance?"

"For instance—" Paul gave Jeremiah a hard, sharp punch in the stomach that caught him by surprise. The pistol fell from his hand and he dropped to his knees, the wind knocked out of him, his eyes wide.

"Then when you're down," Paul went on, "somebody might use a knee on you." He swung his knee at Jeremiah's head, but Jeremiah lurched to the side. The major force of the blow missed its mark, but Jeremiah's face was scraped badly by the rough material of Paul's trousers. "Then maybe a kick," Paul continued, and he kicked hard into Jeremiah's stomach, sending new pain surging through his body and again knocking out what little air had returned to his lungs.

Jeremiah instinctively grabbed the deputy's boot and gave it a desperate twist. Paul fell, cursing. He wasn't hurt, but he was furious at Jeremiah's success. The two men rose to their feet, Paul seething in anger, Jeremiah still trying to get his breath back.

"So," Paul said. "Throw me, huh? You're gonna regret that." He feinted with his right, and Jeremiah ducked right into Paul's left fist coming up the other side. His head snapped back. Paul jabbed at Jeremiah's head with both fists, driving him backward. As Jeremiah got his hands to his face, Paul pounded him in the stomach.

Once Jeremiah struck out blindly with first one hand and then the other, but Paul ducked the first one and easily parried the second. Then he rained a new series of blows on Jeremiah's head and belly.

Jeremiah crumpled to the ground, unable to absorb further punishment, defiant though he felt. Paul grabbed him by the shirtfront and pulled him part way off the ground.

"I saw you with your hands on Anita, Bacon," Paul growled. "Maybe you didn't get the message before. She's mine, understand? Anita's my woman. Every time I see you with that filly," he threatened, "I'm gonna make you wish you tried a different stable." Once more he smashed his fist into Jeremiah's face, knocking him flat on his back in the dust.

Paul picked up Jeremiah's Colt. "Just so you don't get an idea about puttin' a bullet in my back, Bacon, I'm gonna leave your gun at the corner underneath the boardwalk." With a final kick at Jeremiah's stomach, he turned and walked toward the main street, whistling to himself.

Jeremiah wasn't sure how long he lay in the dirt. The next thing he was aware of was the dark sky full of stars, just like he'd seen the first night in Point of Rocks. The whole sky rotated fiercely, though, and he clung to the ground in an effort to make the earth stand still.

He breathed in painful bursts, gagging on warm blood that gurgled in his throat. His lips were cracked, his nose was plastered with dried blood, and his face suffered from many cuts and bruises. His ribs hurt, his stomach felt like someone had fired a cannonball into it, his jaw felt like it was on crooked, and all his bones ached.

He got painfully to his hands and knees, trying to get his balance. Slowly he rose to his feet and stood there panting. The handkerchief from his pocket was soon covered with blood. As each wound stung from the touch of the cloth, he cursed Paul. And he was disgusted with himself for letting the other man get the drop on him. He should have suspected the deputy. He was just too trusting—or too stupid.

Damn that Paul, he had no business working him over like that! If Anita had taken a shine to Jeremiah that was her prerogative, not subject to Paul's veto. And Jeremiah was damned if he'd let anyone tell him whom he could or could not be attracted to. He'd grown powerfully fond of Anita in the short time he'd known her. No way was Paul going to keep them apart if they wanted to be together.

Jeremiah reached the first boardwalk, and he stooped down and peered under the boards. The blood rushed to his head, and he closed his eyes to adjust to the pain. He pawed under the boards until he found his gun. He stood, dusted off the pistol, and inserted it into the holster. Then he walked slowly down the boardwalk of the main street, heading for the Wells Fargo office and his room.

CHAPTER FIFTEEN

Monday, June 27, 1880

"Jeremiah," Anita said urgently, shaking the sleeping man. "Wake up."

"Mmph?" Jeremiah opened his eyes and focused them with difficulty on the woman standing over him. "Anita," he said, surprised to see her.

"I thought you were getting ready, Jeremiah."

"What time is it?"

"Almost eight o'clock," she informed him. "Herb has the stage all set. It's almost ready to leave."

"Oh, my God," he said. He swung his feet off the cot. The sudden movement brought a sharp pain to his head, which reminded him why he hadn't had the energy to get undressed the night before. He grimaced.

"What happened to you?" Anita asked, concerned.

"I had a disagreement with a fellow last night," he answered, realizing she wouldn't have believed he'd had a fall any more than Stacey had believed him Thursday. He cradled his head in his hands.

"Paul again?"

He looked up at her. "Again?"

"I saw what he did when you left the house Wednesday."

"Oh," he said, ashamed. "Well, I guess I'm not much of a man when it comes to fists."

Anita suddenly realized the damage she'd done to his ego by telling him she'd seen him beaten. She changed the subject. "Passengers are coming in, Jeremiah. You might have time to shave."

Jeremiah nodded.

She went to the door and stopped. She bit her lip, then turned around. "Jeremiah."

"Yes?"

"Talk to Herb," she suggested with trepidation. "He's good with his fists."

Jeremiah smiled, much to Anita's relief. "Thanks," he said.

"I'll see that bet, Jer," Herb said, plinking another chip into the pot in the center of the table in the South Pass City saloon.

"I'll see you and raise you two bits, sonny," Vern said with a smile. He tossed two chips into the pile.

Jeremiah gulped and looked at his hand again. A pair of queens and a pair of threes. Not too bad so far for five card draw, but what did Vern have?

Billy Morrison, the next player, sighed and tossed his cards facedown on the table. "I'm out. Not my night, I guess," he said. He pushed his chair back and started to get up.

"Well, I'm still in," Eldon said defiantly. "And I'll raise that another two bits." Three more chips clattered into the pot.

Jeremiah considered. Another fifty cents. "I'll see you," he said and tossed in two chips.

"Hey, Billy," Herb called. "Another bottle."

"You're going to be able to float to Lander tomorrow, Herb," Jeremiah jested.

"Listen, Jer," Herb said, taking the bottle from Billy's hand. "At home I don't drink at all. Sally means too much to me. But out here, I'm still a free man." He popped the cork off the bottle. "Don't worry. A good night's sleep and I'm good as new."

"C'mon, Herb," Eldon scolded. "Your bet."

"Oh, sorry, gents," Herb replied. "I'll see the bets." He plopped in his chips.

"Me, too," Vern said and put in another chip.

"Cards?" Eldon asked.

"One," Jeremiah said. Eldon dealt him another card, a queen.

Herb asked for two cards and tossed away his discards. Eldon slicked two cards off the top of the deck and sailed them across the table. Herb looked at the cards, saying nothing.

"One for me," Vern said. Jeremiah eyed him cautiously, and the miner returned the stare.

"Dealer takes three," Eldon said, dealing off the cards for himself. He paused. "Jeremiah, your bet."

Jeremiah studied his cards carefully. It was the best hand he'd had all night, a full house. "Fifty cents," he challenged as he threw in two chips.

Herb whistled. "Big move by the new jehu. Hmm. Guess I'll stay in." He tossed in two chips.

Vern looked Jeremiah in the eye. "See you," he said, counting out chips, "and raise you a dollar."

"A dollar!" Herb exclaimed.

"Ah, the hell with it," Eldon said, flipping his cards facedown on the table.

Jeremiah ran his finger along the top edge of his cards. "Okay," he said. Here's a dollar and a dollar more."

"Two dollars!" Herb exclaimed, louder. "Hell, you two are bluffin'." He tossed in his chips.

"How much you got in your stack there, sonny?" Vern asked.

Jeremiah glanced at the pitiful stack of chips in front of him. "A dollar seventy-five."

"See you and raise you a dollar seventy-five," Vern said.

"Hell, Vern," Herb said, "you're cleanin' the poor kid out."

"He's lucky I didn't go no higher," Vern countered.

Jeremiah took a deep breath, held it a moment, then pushed the stack into the pot.

"Wow, you desert sidewinders play for keeps," Herb

commented. "Well, what the hell. I still think you're bluffin'." He tossed the appropriate number of chips into the growing pile in the center of the table.

Jeremiah spread his cards on the table in front of him. "Queens full," he said smugly.

Vern snickered. He laid his cards down slowly for full dramatic effect. "Kings full," he said triumphantly.

Jeremiah was crushed. Vern, giggling with delight, reached for the pot.

"I got eight," Herb said.

Vern stopped. "What d'ya mean ya got 'eight?'"

"Two, four, six, eight," Herb counted out, and he flipped the four deuces consecutively onto the table.

"Hell and damnation," Vern swore, looking at the cards.

Herb laughed and gathered in the pot. Both Vern and Jeremiah stared enviously at the man.

"I'm busted," Jeremiah said. "Guess I'll hit the sack—where I should have been a long time ago."

"Okay, Jer," Herb said. "I'll see you later. Hope you liked the poker lesson."

Jeremiah got up. "It's one I won't soon forget," he said. "See you later, Herb. Bye, Eldon, Vern." The two men addressed nodded a farewell, and Jeremiah headed for the door. "Night, Billy," he said to the man behind the bar.

"Night, Jeremiah," Billy replied.

A crashing thud woke Jeremiah. He jerked his head up and peered around the room. Through the darkness he could make out the form of a man struggling to get up off the floor.

"Herb?"

"Shhh," the man on the floor cautioned. "Don' wanna wake Jer," he slurred.

Jeremiah got out of bed and padded over to where Herb was sprawled. He tried to pull him up. Awkwardly he got Herb to his feet and then steered him to the bed, on which the man flopped unceremoniously. "Oh, boy, what a night," Herb commented. "You lef' too soon, Jer. I coulda staked ya."

"No, thanks," Jeremiah said, glad to have cut his losses when he did. "Who won in the end?"

"Why, hell, Eldon and Billy, 'course," Herb said. "They always win."

"Why? Do they cheat?"

"Naw," Herb scoffed and laughed. "Jus' that 'fore ya get outa the saloon, ya've either los' all your money at cards or spent it all on that rotgut liquor o' theirs." He sighed. "Damn. Won myself a horse tonigh', too."

"You won a horse?" Jeremiah asked. "Why, that's great."

"Los' 'im again. Another fella came in, see. Los' all his money 'n' put 'is horse up. I won!" Herb laughed. "Then he pu' his Winches'er and saddle up agin the horse and all my money. Dammit! Cleaned me out."

Jeremiah couldn't help but laugh.

Herb sighed. "A beaut of a horse, too. Black wi' white stockin's."

Jeremiah's scalp cringed. One of his father's murderers had ridden a horse like that. "Herb," he said. "Was he short? With black hair and sort of a long face?"

"Black Herb thought a moment. "Yeah, 'course. But tall, not short."

Jeremiah was deflated. "Did he have a mustache?"

Herb laughed. "Hell, who ever seen a horse with a mustache?"

"Not the horse, Herb," Jeremiah said in exasperation. "The man. What did the man look like?"

"Oh, ah—well. Black hair, mustache. And he was shor' like ya say. With eyes—"

"Is he still in the saloon, Herb?" Jeremiah interrupted.

"He was fixin' to leave. No more money," he said and laughed loudly.

Jeremiah frantically pulled on his pants, sat on the bed, and rammed his feet into his boots. He rushed out of the room, along the hall, down the stairs, and out the door of the hotel.

Just as he hit the boardwalk, the short, black-haired man came out of the saloon, turned and called a farewell to the men inside. Jeremiah immediately recognized him, and he went for his gun.

Jeremiah swore when his hand hit his pants where the pistol should have been. It was still in its holster upstairs in the hotel room. He watched helplessly as the outlaw mounted the black horse, turned him, and headed slowly down the street.

Jeremiah ran into the saloon. "That man who was just in here," he said breathlessly. "He's one of the men who killed my father!"

"What? You sure?" Billy asked.

"Yes, I saw him that night in the light from a window," Jeremiah confirmed. "Get your guns and horses; we can still catch him."

"Whoa there, Jeremiah," Eldon said. "That's a job for the law."

"The law! That man could be two states away by the time the law gets here!"

"He didn't seem to be going anywhere in particular," Billy said. "Besides, I haven't fired a gun in years," he added apologetically.

Jeremiah stared at the two men, incredulous, clenching and unclenching his fists. Vern was no longer in the saloon. Jeremiah turned and ran back to the hotel, took the stairs three steps at a time, and ran to his room.

"Herb!" he called. "That man was one of the men who killed my father. We have to go after him."

"Mm?"

"Get your gun, Herb," Jeremiah pleaded. He pulled the man upright on the bed.

"Gun," Herb said. "Right. Gun, gun, gun."

"Herb!" Jeremiah shook him. "Wake up, Herb!"

"Right," Herb mumbled. His head dropped, and he started snoring instantly.

Jeremiah let him down slowly. "Oh, Herb," he said. He took a deep breath. Then he stood, grabbed his shirt, vest, and hat, buckled on his holster, retrieved Herb's Winchester from against the wall, and grabbed a box of cartridges. Then he headed for the door and the corral in back of the blacksmith's shop.

At the shop, he paused to put his shirt and vest on. Then he grabbed a bridle from inside the unlocked shed and put it on one of the stage horses. He didn't bother with a saddle.

A half-moon enabled Jeremiah to spot the outlaw not far from town; the man was in no hurry. He rode his black horse for half an hour until he arrived at a smoldering campfire located along a creek. He unsaddled the horse, hobbled it, and then spread a bedroll down in front of his overturned saddle.

Jeremiah tied his horse to a sagebrush bush behind a small hill and caressed the velvety muzzle of the animal. Then, Winchester in hand, he crawled to the top of the rise and surveyed the camp below. The outlaw was alone, unsuspecting, and turning in for the night.

Jeremiah waited another half hour to make sure the man was asleep. Then he cautiously approached the camp. It was incredible how loud walking on sand sounded to him. Reaching the sleeping man, he gingerly reached down and pulled the outlaw's gun from its holster underneath the saddle. He gave the man a light kick.

"You're under arrest!" he shouted.

The man jumped awake and reached for his gun. He saw the barrel of the Winchester pointed at him, and he froze.

"Who're you?" he demanded to know.

"My name's Jeremiah Bacon, and I'm making a citizen's arrest to take you back to hang for the murder of my father and Cyrus Kessler."

The outlaw swallowed and stared at the carbine's muzzle.

"Saddle your horse," Jeremiah ordered.

"Knowed I should've stayed away from town," the man said, flipping the blanket aside and getting slowly to his feet. He bent down and pulled up the blanket. "Mind if I roll up my blanket?"

"Go ahead," Jeremiah said.

The man seized the blanket by two edges and jiggled it in front of him, trying to get the other edges to line up. Too late Jeremiah saw the trap. The blanket came sailing through the air, and Jeremiah fired. The noise was deafening in the still night.

The blanket fell to the ground, and a bewildered Jeremiah had the wind knocked out of him when the outlaw plowed into him from the side. The men went down. The barrel of the Winchester dug into the ground, and Jeremiah's fingers were torn, cracking and complaining from the lever of the carbine. The outlaw's pistol was knocked from his other hand as well.

"You little greenhorn bastard," the outlaw snarled at him as the two men rolled in the sand. "Thought you could take ol' Cleve, did you?"

As they struggled, Jeremiah fumbled for his own gun, but only succeeded in losing that one, too. And Cleve was a good deal stronger than Jeremiah even if he was shorter, so Jeremiah was once more getting the worst of a fight.

The outlaw threw Jeremiah aside, and both men got to their feet quickly. Jeremiah was aghast. Again his thirst for vengeance had gotten him into big trouble. Again fear of death clutched his heart. But this time MacKenzie would not be around.

Cleve reached into his boot and pulled out a knife. "See this, kid?" he asked through a rasping breath. "I'm gonna stick it in your belly and pull it out through the ribs in your back."

Jeremiah backed up warily as the other man started toward him, crouching, hefting the knife in his hand.

Jeremiah's eyes hunted longingly for a gun, but all he could see in the dark was the Winchester—on the other side of Cleve. Jeremiah continued backing up.

"That's it, my hero," the man taunted, enjoying his supremacy. He lunged with the knife, sweeping it in a wide arc in front of Jeremiah's face. Jeremiah leaped backward. The man laughed gleefully. "Close?" he asked, smiling. "Did you see that little snake flick its tongue at you? Well, it bites, too."

Cleve lunged again, and the keen blade effortlessly cut a gash across Jeremiah's arm. The blood flowed quickly and started to ooze between the fingers of the hand Jeremiah clamped over the wound. The warm touch of his own blood panicked Jeremiah. He broke and ran.

"It's no good runnin'!" Cleve shouted. Jeremiah turned just in time to see the man hurl the knife at him. He swerved and heard the deadly missile whiz past his head.

The outlaw swore in disgust, then started after Jeremiah, bellowing his anger. "I'll kill you with my bare hands!"

Jeremiah ran blindly, stumbling through the sandy soil, crashing through the sagebrush. His ankle twisted on a rock, and he fell on his face, eyes shut in pain.

"Got you now, you bastard!" Cleve whooped in triumph.

Jeremiah opened his eyes. Cleve's knife lay in front of his face. He grabbed it and rolled to his right, just as the outlaw roared and leaped for him. Jeremiah brought the knife up hard. The sharp blade punched easily through the man's stomach wall, slicing a long path through the membranes and internal organs, lodging finally deep inside the man's abdomen.

Jeremiah gasped and released the knife, appalled. The outlaw contorted his body in a stiff, arching motion, raising his belly off the sand and then flopping onto his side. "I—didn't—see . . ."

Jeremiah got to his feet quickly and backed off, staring at the man and wiping his hands on his pants.

The outlaw forced himself to sit up, sobbing with effort. "Damn you," he growled.

"I didn't mean to . . ." Jeremiah started, but felt ridiculous, for he had meant to do exactly that.

"Hell, you say," the outlaw snapped. His hand closed around the handle of the knife, and he drew it slowly out of his wound, then let it drop to the ground.

"I'll get you back to town," Jeremiah said. "They can fix you up there."

"For what? Fix my guts so I can swing from a rope?" Cleve clutched his stomach with both hands.

"I'll get your horse," Jeremiah said quietly.

The man chuckled sardonically. "Bounce my guts out, too, huh?"

Jeremiah started backing away. He wiped his face and then stuck a handkerchief into the tear in his sleeve in an effort to stanch the flow of blood from the knife wound. He limped to where the man had left his horse, and he saddled the animal as rapidly as his wound and ineptness would allow. After a short search, he gathered the two pistols and the Winchester, and then coaxed the unhobbled horse toward the spot where he'd left Cleve.

The wounded man was lying on his back, his hands still pressed tightly to his stomach.

"I got your horse," Jeremiah said.

Cleve didn't move. Jeremiah knelt down and felt for the man's pulse in his wrist, then in his jugular vein. There was none.

Jeremiah stood up slowly.

"That's two," he declared solemnly.

Then he walked a few paces to the side and vomited into a greasewood bush.

CHAPTER SIXTEEN

Tuesday, June 28, 1880

Jeremiah was relieved to drive the stage onto the dark street of South Pass City after a long day of driving. He stopped the stage in front of the hotel, where Eldon stood waiting, and wrapped the reins around the brake handle. Herb and he struggled to haul the strong box from its awkward place in the boot.

"Big shipment?" Eldon asked.

"Near ten thousand," Herb answered. Jeremiah handed the box down to Eldon, and the latter carried the box with the gold from the Atlantic City mines into the lobby. Jeremiah climbed down and opened the door for their sole passenger, a man from Thermopolis headed for Green River. Herb took the mail-pouch into the hotel.

Herb and Jeremiah took the stage to the blacksmith's shop, unhitched it, and settled the horses in the corral. Then they joined Eldon and the passenger in the hotel dining room. Dinner was quick.

"Let's step out back, Jer," Herb said, pushing his chair back.

"No saloon tonight?" Jeremiah asked.

"Not yet. Tonight you get that lesson in the manly art of self defense you wanted."

"Okay."

"First," Herb said, walking to the kitchen, "grab yourself a couple o' towels. Here." He went to a rack where some towels hung. He threw two of them to Jeremiah, and then blew a kiss toward the cook when she scowled at them.

"Do we really need these?" Jeremiah asked.

"The only way you're gonna learn to fight is to actually fight," Herb explained. "But there's no need o' hurtin' each other *too* much."

"Makes sense," Jeremiah said. His head was in bad enough shape as it was.

The two men exited through the back door of the hotel and walked onto the bare ground that separated the hotel from Willow Creek. Herb, tightening the towels he had wrapped around his hands, approached Jeremiah. "Okay," he said, "defend yourself." He shot a jab at Jeremiah's head. Jeremiah turned his head and managed to get both hands in front of his face, deflecting the blow.

"Oh, Jesus," Herb said. "You *do* need help."

"I stopped you from hitting me," Jeremiah pointed out.

"You had your eyes closed! You looked away, and you put both your hands up in front of your face," Herb criticized.

"So?"

"Try it again." Jeremiah prepared for Herb's jab and again he ducked and successfully blocked Herb's attack. But Herb deftly punched him in the stomach, and Jeremiah's breath left him with an "Oof!"

"You see?" Herb asked. "You left yourself wide open."

Jeremiah massaged his stomach. "I see," he managed to squeak out.

"And you grabbed your stomach and left your face unprotected after I hit you," Herb continued. "I'd have smashed it in."

Jeremiah straightened up painfully. "So what do I do?"

"Rule number one," Herb announced. "Never take your eyes off the other guy. If he aims for your face, block the jab, but always keep lookin' him in the eye. Try it. I'll jab, you block. But keep lookin'."

Herb jabbed at Jeremiah a number of times, and Jeremiah, under Herb's encouragement, was able to overcome his strong tendency to close his eyes and duck.

"Okay," Herb said. "You're gettin' that pretty good. Now let's do somethin' 'bout your hands."

"What's wrong with them?"

"You've got 'em bunched together," Herb said. "Hold your hands like this. One leadin', the jabber," he described as he demonstrated with his own hands, "the other trailin', hidin' your face, the blocker. One for offense, the other for defense." Jeremiah copied his stance. "Good," Herb judged. "Now practice some jabs. Short, hard, and sharp. Not sledgehammers; save that for a real good openin'. But keep punchin' the other guy all the time to keep him occupied. Try it," he said, holding up a hand.

Jeremiah jabbed at it.

"Well, don't be a butterfly 'bout it," Herb scolded. "You gotta hit hard enough to get his attention. Harder, harder. Short snap, then return. Jab again."

Jeremiah practiced that for a short time, jabbing repeatedly at Herb's upheld hand.

"Okay, now some combinations," Herb said. "The ol' one-two. Jab to the head, then the belly. Jus' like I caught you before."

Jeremiah went through the motions, a jab at Herb's head, which he easily blocked, and then a punch at Herb's stomach, which he also easily blocked.

"Gotta be faster, Jer," Herb said. "And really try to hit me, that's the only way you'll get the right feel for it."

"I don't want to hurt you," Jeremiah said, voicing his reluctance.

"Don't worry," Herb assured him, smiling. "You won't."

Jeremiah concentrated. He jabbed at Herb's head and then directed a blow at the other man's stomach. Herb cuffed him on the side of head.

"Hey!" Jeremiah exclaimed. "That wasn't fair."

"Couple more rules," Herb said. "Always protect yourself, even when you're lettin' the other guy have it. And learn to anticipate, figure out where the other guy is gonna leave himself open. But watch out you don't leave yourself open. When you went for my gut, you dropped your other hand, left your head unprotected. Bring the other hand up like this when you reach out with the first one." He demonstrated. "Try it again."

The two men went through the exercise repeatedly, Jeremiah trying to hit Herb, and Herb parrying the thrusts and snapping back at Jeremiah, teaching him to guard himself. After that, Herb showed him other combinations and punches.

"When you see an opportunity—jus' a split second is all it takes—than let 'im have the ol' haymaker," Herb counseled. "Aim for the head; it's easier to hurt a man in the head than in the stomach. There's no fat to cushion the blow. And aim for the back of the head, from the front. That way you won't let up too soon. Follow through all the way." He glanced at Jeremiah's hands. "And another thing, 'specially for you. You can't worry 'bout your hands in a fight. You gotta worry 'bout hurtin' the other guy. If your hands are all beat outa shape, that means the other guy is, too."

Jeremiah thought of his hands yet again. Already they were bruised, cut, callused, blistered, scraped, and torn. What would happen to them if he stayed in Point of Rocks much longer?

"Okay," Herb said. "Tell you what. Let's pretend I'm Paul Warner, and we're havin' another to do."

The two men squared off, shuffling about each other. Herb would jab at Jeremiah, feint, and jab again. Jeremiah copied his movements and tried to use the same technique himself.

"Use all your strength, Jer," Herb said. "Only way you're gonna learn."

Jeremiah tried the best he could to get at Herb, but the older man was quick and experienced. Frustration mounted as time and again Jeremiah would direct what he thought would be a telling blow only to have it parried. And Herb would clout him in return. Herb chuckled and laughed, taunting and teasing.

Jeremiah was fast losing his endurance. He couldn't believe how Herb managed to go on with hardly a sign of fatigue. And the man's constant barrage of both laughter and insults began to infuriate him, even though he realized Herb was doing it only to goad him on to his best.

But Jeremiah was learning. He was getting at Herb. Herb complimented him on several good blows, and Jeremiah was gratified, though he worried when Herb staggered.

Jeremiah saw an opening, a momentary laxness in Herb's guard. He pictured Paul standing there. With all the strength he could muster he smashed Herb on the jaw, snapping his head back and throwing the teacher backward, stumbling until he fell.

"My God!" Jeremiah gasped, startled at the effect on the man. "I'm sorry, Herb." He rushed over, stripping the towels from his hands. "Did I hurt you?"

"Hell, yes," Herb declared, carefully feeling his jaw. "It was beautiful."

"God, I'm sorry, Herb."

"Don't be," Herb soothed. "It means I taught you good."

Jeremiah felt elated. "I can't wait to get another crack at that deputy."

"Don't be anxious for a fight, Jer," Herb cautioned. "Paul's still a lot better than you are. He's had a lot more experience. And remember, in a fight, even the winner usually comes out bloody and bruised."

"Paul didn't," Jeremiah said.

"I said a fight," Herb emphasized, "not a whippin'."

Jeremiah understood perfectly.

"Ooo," Herb moaned. "Help me to my feet, Jer. I wanna go soak my head in the creek."

CHAPTER SEVENTEEN

Wednesday, June 29, 1880

The day was already warm when the stage left South
Pass City, with a clear sky giving the sun an unob-
structed view of the countryside. And Jeremiah was
even more uncomfortable with the body of the outlaw he had killed,. trussed in canvas, tied securely
to the top of the coach. Jeremiah felt like he was driving a hearse rather than a stagecoach.

The stage crossed the Sweetwater River, changed
teams at the swing station there, and then headed
southward into the hills. Jeremiah had barely settled
into the routine of the drive when he was confronted
at a sharp curve by a man on horseback planted
squarely in the middle of the road. The rider wore a
white duster, and pulled over his head was a sack with
eye-and-mouth holes cut in it. The man waved a gun
in the air. "Pull up!"

Herb reached for his Winchester A warning volley
of rifle fire crackled along the ridges on either side
of the road, and bullets kicked up dirt alongside the
stage. Herb froze. Jeremiah brought the stage to a
quick stop, with the leaders no more than three feet
from where the outlaw's horse was prancing.

"Toss the hardware in the dirt, gents," the horsemen
ordered. Jeremiah recognized the voice immediately,
the gravel-throated voice that he could never forget.

"Herb," he said emphatically. "It's him!"

"The Red Desert Gang, Jer," Herb said. He pitched
the Winchester off the stage, then reached for his pistol and threw that after the carbine. Jeremiah tossed

his pistol to the ground and then sat shifting the reins in his hands nervously.

"The express box, shotgun," the outlaw demanded.

"They knew, Herb," Jeremiah said.

"They always do," the other man declared disgustedly. He reached down into the boot and pulled up the strong box, then heaved it to the ground.

The outlaw walked his horse toward the box. "Anybody who moves," he warned, "catches a rifle slug." He peered into the interior of the stagecoach but showed no interest in the passenger; who sat there docilely. Then he returned to the strong box, dismounted, took aim with his pistol and shot off the lock. His horse shied, but the man kept a firm hold on the reins. Jeremiah held the stage horses in check.

The lid of the box was flipped open, revealing four bags. The outlaw holstered his gun and reached in with both hands, coming up with a bag in each of them. He stuck them into his saddlebags and then returned for the other two bags, stowing them alongside the first two.

. The man closed the lid, picked up the box, and tossed it up to Herb. "Thanks," he said mockingly. Herb dropped the box back into the boot, and the outlaw remounted.

"Who's in the bag?" the hooded man asked, pointing with the pistol he had drawn again.

Jeremiah felt a new fear run through him. What would happen if the outlaw discovered it was one of his gang in the bag?

"A miner," Herb lied.

"What are you takin' him to Point of Rocks for?"

Jeremiah was relieved; the outlaw was ignorant of the body's real identity.

"Family wants him buried in Green River," Herb lied further.

"They better hurry with this sun." He looked at both men on the stage. "You're Jeremiah Bacon, aren't you?" he asked, pointing his pistol at Jeremiah.

Jeremiah gulped. "Yes," he said hesitantly. "I'm Jeremiah Bacon."

"Mm." The outlaw cocked the hammer of his pistol, raised the revolver slightly, and then fired. Jeremiah's head spun around as Herb lurched backward, his hands and head thrown back, his feet straining against the foot rest of the driver's seat. The outlaw fired again, and the impact knocked Herb off the seat. He landed on the ground with a sickening crunch.

Jeremiah was horrified. He dropped the reins, even though the horses threatened to bolt. His lips quivered, and he looked at the outlaw, enraged.

"Why the hell did you do that!" Jeremiah demanded to know. "You had the money!" he shouted. "You didn't have to shoot anybody. You bastard!"

The outlaw laughed. "Be seein' you, Bacon." Still laughing, he turned his horse and urged him up the hill.

Jeremiah whirled and leaped from the driver's seat, landing close to Herb. The passenger was climbing out of the coach.

"They shot him!" Jeremiah said, almost shouting at the man. "They shot him in cold blood!"

"I've never heard of anything like this," the man said. "There was no cause for it."

The two men knelt over Herb and both tried to find signs of life, but failed.

"He's dead," Jeremiah said softly, looking up at the passenger. "Herb is dead." Jeremiah could not believe it. "Why?" he asked. "For God's sake, why?"

The news spread rapidly through Point of Rocks, and, late though it was, a sizable crowd gathered about the Wells Fargo office after the stage arrived that night. The people stood about, some in the street, some on the boardwalks, mumbling to each other and gawking at the spectacle. Taylor Pierce directed several men in loading the two bodies onto a wagon for the short trip to his undertaking parlor.

"Bacon," Otis MacKenzie said, "I'm going with Pierce. Meet me over at the jail later I want to talk to you about this some more."

"Why don't you go after the men who did it?" Jeremiah asked, irritated.

"Look," Otis explained patiently "Herb Lambrecht was a good friend of mine. I knew him a lot longer than you did, and I want to catch the men who did this just as much as you do. But this happened twelve hours, thirteen hours ago. There's no chance of catchin' up with 'em. They've long since scuttled off to whatever holes they hide in."

Jeremiah fumed but realized the marshal was quite right. He nodded. "I know, I know," he said. "It's just that . . ."

Otis patted him on the shoulder sympathetically, then joined Pierce on the wagon. They set off for the shop. Seth drove the stage away from the office, and the crowd began dispersing. Jeremiah went into the office where he found Anita examining a ledger.

"Anita," he said quietly.

The young woman looked up, and Jeremiah noted the tears that had started down her cheeks. "I—was just going through the records," she said, her voice choked, "figuring out how much we owe Sally for Herb's work."

Jeremiah nodded. "I knew Herb only a short time, but . . ."

"He was a good man," Anita pronounced. "Like my father. And yours." She slowly closed the cover of the ledger. "Oh, Jeremiah," she said sadly, "won't the killing ever stop? I'm so tired of death. So many good people have died."

"It'll stop, Anita," Jeremiah reassured her. "It'll stop when that whole gang is rounded up and hanged. And particularly the leader. Get him and the rest will fade away."

She came around from in back of the counter.

"Maybe the line ought to be closed. All the killing's been connected in some way with Wells Fargo."

"Close it down?" Jeremiah asked, surprised. "You can't do that. The town needs this line. *You* need this line. It's not fair that a gang of murderers determine its fate."

"Fair?" The young woman paused and walked toward the window facing the street. "Life isn't fair," she observed, peering into the darkness. "It's just more unfair to some than to others."

Jeremiah came up behind her. "I won't let you quit," he said firmly. "I'll get those men. I'll put a stop to the killing."

Anita turned and smiled at him. "The marshal's been trying to do that for almost three years," she pointed out.

"I've already gotten two of them," Jeremiah said. "That's better than the marshal's done."

Anita raised her eyebrows. "True," she admitted. "But that's not the marshal's fault. He's a good man, too."

"Then you won't drop the stage line?"

"Well, with Herb gone now—"

"I'll drive the stage both runs," Jeremiah volunteered.

"Think you can handle the stage alone now?" she asked.

"With both hands tied behind my back," he boasted. "I drove it here, didn't I?"

"What about the piano playing, the saloon job?"

"Forget it," Jeremiah said. "I can play the piano in my spare time, and this job pays more, anyway."

Anita smiled. "Okay, whip," she said.

"Okay, boss," he answered. Their eyes met and lingered. "Well," he broke off, "the marshal wanted to see me."

Anita nodded and stood aside. Jeremiah picked up Herb's Winchester.

"I'd be real proud to have this Winchester of Herb's, Anita. Could you ask his widow if she'd consider parting with it? I'd be willing to pay well, though I can't pay all of it right away."

"I'll ask her."

"Good. Well, 'til tomorrow morning," he said and headed for the door. He rested the Winchester against the wall. "I'd walk you home but . . ."

"I'll be all right. Good night, Jeremiah."

"Good night, Anita."

Jeremiah opened the door and stepped out. He stopped when he saw Paul Warner leaning against a post in front of the general store across the street. Jeremiah paused, then turned and walked back into the office.

"Something wrong, Jeremiah?" Anita asked from the counter where she'd gone to pick up a shawl.

"Anita," he said simply. He seized her gently but firmly by the shoulders, pulled her to him, and gave her a long passionate kiss. She struggled initially but quickly relented.

"Jeremiah Bacon!" she scolded mildly when he released her. She looked furtively out the window. "The idea! Right where people can see."

"I know."

She looked at him, puzzled.

"Good night, Anita," he said again. He gave her hand a long gentle squeeze.

"Good night, Jeremiah," she said sweetly.

Jeremiah left the office and headed for the jail. Anita closed up the office and locked it, then headed down the street, humming to herself, a little skip to her walk.

Jeremiah opened the door of the marshal's office. As he had expected, Paul was waiting, standing in the middle of the floor, his feet apart, his thumbs hooked into his gunbelt.

"Evening, Paul," Jeremiah said with forced politeness. He closed the door and hung his hat on a peg on the back of the door. He turned to face the deputy.

"I guess you don't learn so good," Paul said.

"Learn what?"

"That Anita Kessler is mine," the man said sternly. "You're trespassin' on my property."

"I'd say she's drawn the property lines a little differently," Jeremiah countered.

Paul pulled a pair of gloves out of his back pocket and made a great show of putting them on, smoothing the leather carefully to fit the contours of his fingers.

"You going to shoot me?" Jeremiah asked.

"Not tonight," the deputy said. "Tonight I'm just gonna beat the hell outa you." He tossed his hat on a chair and walked up to Jeremiah. Without further preliminaries he cocked his arm back and aimed a hard punch at Jeremiah's head.

Jeremiah deftly parried the thrust, and his eyes concentrated on Paul's face as he aimed for the back of his head—from the front. There was a loud *clack* as Paul's teeth collided with each other. The deputy reeled backward and he fell over a chair, landing on the floor in a heap.

Paul looked at Jeremiah with a stunned look on his face. "You lucky bastard," he snarled. He leaped to his feet and charged, swinging wildly.

Jeremiah exploited Paul's frenzy and his resulting carelessness to pepper his head with telling jabs. And when Paul went to guard his face, Jeremiah worked over his stomach. Paul backed away, his nose sniffling to suppress the flow of blood and dabbing at more of the precious fluid that trickled from his mouth and a cut over one eye. He examined the red streaks on his glove with amazed disbelief.

Jeremiah saw his opportunity and swung with all his might. The blow caught Paul on the side of the head, and he staggered backward into the wall. Jeremiah leaped up to him and swung again and again at Paul's head, knocking it first one way, and then the other. Paul threw himself on Jeremiah in desperation, and the two danced out into the middle of the room before Jeremiah could free himself. Paul stood there swaying, and Jeremiah put all he had into a punch to the deputy's stomach. The man doubled up, holding his belly with both hands.

Jeremiah put a boot to Paul's shoulder and gave a shove. The deputy flew backward, his hands clutching the air. He landed against the edge of the desk, grimaced, and sank to the floor. He moaned and mumbled to himself and rolled over till he was on his back. He glared malevolently at Jeremiah, and his hand crept down for his forty-five.

Jeremiah saw the motion and his hand started for his own gun slowly.

The door of the office opened, and Otis MacKenzie stepped in. He recognized the sign of imminent gunplay, and his hand went for his well-used six-gun. "What's going on here?" he asked. He pondered which one he would shoot.

Jeremiah straightened up, and Paul let his hand fall to the floor. "Paul was giving me a lesson in fistfighting, Marshal," Jeremiah said, "and I returned the favor by showing him some things Herb taught me."

Paul pulled himself up from the floor by grabbing the desktop. He wiped some more blood off onto his sleeve and then staggered over to the chair to retrieve his hat, pushing Jeremiah aside to get to it. He crammed the hat down on his head and left the office sullenly, slamming the door behind him.

"Personal matter?" Otis asked.

"Yes, sir."

"Mm." Otis took off his hat and hung it on a peg next to Jeremiah's. "Pick up the place, will you?" he said to Jeremiah. Jeremiah nodded and began setting up chairs. Otis went to his desk and sat down. Jeremiah finished and pulled up a chair in front of the desk.

"Identified the fellow you killed, Bacon," Otis informed him. "Name's Cleveland Armana. Never seen him in Point of Rocks, but he's been around Lander and South Pass City a bit, presumably cowpunchin' or minin', but now it seems he was doin' otherwise."

"He won't be doing it anymore."

"No, that's for sure." Otis swiveled back and forth in his chair several times. "Did it ever occur to you to try to take the man alive, Bacon?"

"I tried to capture him first," Jeremiah explained, "but like I told you before, he got the drop on me. I'm lucky he didn't kill me."

"That's for sure, too," Otis agreed. "You're the luckiest son of a mustang I've ever seen." Otis slammed his fist down on the desk. "But, dammit, that's twice we had a chance for a solid lead, and you blew it."

"I'm sorry," Jeremiah pleaded earnestly. "Believe me, I'm sorry."

"Hmph," Otis commented. He reached into his drawer and pulled out a bottle and a glass.

"The fifty-dollar reward," Jeremiah mentioned.

"What about it?"

"I'd like it to go to Herb's widow," Jeremiah said.

Otis looked at Jeremiah approvingly. "Consider it done." He pulled the cork out of the bottle with a squeak. "An interesting point about this Armana. He hung around with another fellow—a fellow by the name of Tom."

"Tom!" Jeremiah repeated, sitting upright.

"Yeah, Tom Hocker." Otis poured a glassful of the brown liquid.

"Where can I—we find him?"

"Hell if I'm gonna tell you. You'll just go out and try to kill him."

"How many times do I have to tell you," Jeremiah said in exasperation. "I didn't *intend* to kill Armana."

"So you say."

"You don't believe me?"

"Doesn't matter." Otis took a long drink from the glass.

Jeremiah slumped back in his chair. He looked at

Otis as the man started to fill the glass again. "Can I have one of those?"

Otis spilled some liquor on the desk top. "You want some whiskey?" he asked, looking at the young man in surprise.

"Yes," he answered. "I hear it helps you forget."

The marshal nodded, then retrieved another glass from the desk drawer. He set it down in front of Jeremiah and filled it. Then he picked up his own glass. "A toast," he suggested. "To Herb Lambrecht."

Jeremiah picked up the glass carefully. "To Herb Lambrecht," he repeated. Otis downed the contents of his glass and then watched Jeremiah as the young man brought the glass to his lips, closed his eyes, and gulped down the drink. Finishing, Jeremiah slammed the glass down and screwed up his face in pain.

"My God," he said after catching his breath. "No wonder you forget everything else."

The marshal chuckled. "Another?"

Jeremiah rubbed the tears from his eyes. He blinked and refocused. "Hit me again," he said, "but just a little this time."

An hour later Jeremiah was passing the saloon on his way back to the Wells Fargo office when Zwieg stopped him outside the place. "Jeremiah," the saloon owner said. "Heard about the murder of poor Herb. Terrible thing."

"Yes, sir," Jeremiah agreed sadly.

"Also hear you got one of the outlaws, though," Zwieg added.

"Yes, a fellow by the name of Cleveland Armana."

"Who?" Stacey asked, coming up to the two men.

"Cleveland Armana," Jeremiah repeated. "He's the one I saw in the light from the window the night of the murders."

"Name doesn't ring a bell," Zwieg said. Stacey shrugged her shoulders. "How about a drink to help you relax, Jeremiah?" Zwieg offered. "You've had a damn poor day."

"No, thanks, Mr. Zwieg," Jeremiah said. "I tried that at the marshal's, but it didn't seem to take my mind off things."

"Okay," Zwieg said. "We'll see you 'round." The man took his leave and went back inside.

Stacey put her hands on Jeremiah's shoulders. "I can take your mind off things, Jerry," she said seductively.

Jeremiah looked down into her pretty face and followed the contours of her shoulders. Strangely, the thought of Anita popped into his head, and he was suddenly ambivalent about the prospects of a romp in bed with the saloon girl.

"Thanks for the offer, Stacey," he said, "but I'm so damned tired, I think I'll just hit the hay."

"Well!" she said, dumbfounded at a man declining an opportunity to enjoy her charms—for free, at that. "Suit yourself, honey," she added, a bit miffed.

"Good night, Stacey," he said and pulled away slowly.

"Good night, Jerry," she said and watched him walk away. "If you should change your mind . . ."

CHAPTER EIGHTEEN

Saturday, July 2, 1880

Jeremiah jumped down from the stage in front of the Wells Fargo office, grateful to have finished another round trip. He assisted two passengers in leaving the coach and got their baggage for them.

"How was the trip, Jeremiah?" Anita asked, coming out of the office. She greeted the passengers as they passed, headed for the hotel down the street.

"Oh, not too bad," Jeremiah judged. "A few tight spots. I wished Herb had been along."

Anita nodded sympathetically.

"Odd, Anita," Jeremiah said, smiling. "I found myself talking just like Herb. I told one of the passengers all about Hank Monk and—"

Anita laughed. "Herb's favorite story."

"Yes." Jeremiah laughed himself. He mounted the boot and pulled out the strong box. "Say," he said, descending and carrying it into the office, "did Mac-Kenzie bring anybody in while I was gone?"

"No," she answered, frowning. "Did you expect him to?"

Jeremiah dropped the box behind the counter. "It's empty," he said. "I'm going to talk to the marshal. Seth should be here directly, shouldn't he?" he asked, nodding toward the stagecoach.

"Yes, I'm sure."

"Okay," Jeremiah said, heading for the door. He stopped and looked back at Anita. "See you tomorrow?" he asked hopefully.

"Sure," Anita said. She gave him a big smile. "Noon sharp."

Jeremiah winked and left the office.

He hurried over to the marshal's office, bursting eagerly in through the door and stopping. Otis was sitting at the desk, his feet propped up on it, a glass sitting in front of him next to a bottle, and an open book in his hands.

"Well?" Jeremiah asked.

"Well, what?" Otis asked, looking up from his reading.

"Tom Hocker!" Jeremiah slammed the door shut.

"Gone."

"Gone?" Jeremiah repeated. He walked up to the marshal's desk.

"Just like Gordie," Otis said disgustedly. He closed the book and tossed it on the desk. Jeremiah glanced at the title: *McCoy's Complete Guide to Stock Raising*. "I got to the Lazy F before the prairie larks were up Thursday morning, but he'd already left. Someone rode in a few hours before I did, stayed a few minutes, left, and Hocker left a few minutes after that. I tried to follow him but lost the trail."

"Damn," Jeremiah said. He plunked down into a chair. Then he pulled it closer to the desk, tilted it back on two legs, and propped his feet up the way Otis had his.

"Drink?" Otis offered.

"No thanks," Jeremiah declined. He smiled. "I didn't really appreciate it the other night. Man, my mother would disown me if she knew how many glasses I had."

Otis laughed. "She doesn't approve of hard liquor?"

Jeremiah shook his head. "Beer is almost more than she can tolerate in a man."

"Is that a fact?"

Jeremiah sighed. "I guess getting Hocker was too much to hope for."

Otis corked the bottle and put it away. He rose and

walked a few paces off. "The thing I don't understand is, who warned him? Who knew I was going out there? How many people knew it was Cleveland Armana you killed? Well—Pierce was the only one besides me to see the body in Point of Rocks. I don't think he knew Armana, and I didn't tell him who it was. So the gang leader couldn't have learned here in town that it was Armana you brought in. And yet, if he had gotten any information from South Pass City, why would he've waited so long to warn Hocker?" Otis stopped his pacing and looked suspiciously at Jeremiah. "Did you tell anybody it was Armana you killed?"

"Of course not," Jeremiah said quickly. Then he froze. He lifted his feet off the desk and let the chair drop. "Oh, my God," he said.

"What's the matter?" Otis asked.

"Zwieg," Jeremiah said simply.

"What about him?"

"I told Zwieg about Armana," Jeremiah elaborated. "Right after I left here."

"Why'd you do that?" Otis asked impatiently.

"Well, I didn't exactly have my head on straight when I left here Wednesday," he excused himself, waving toward the drawer containing the bottle of liquor.

"Did Zwieg know that Armana was the one you saw in the light and that he called the other fellow chasing you 'Tom'?"

"Yes," Jeremiah confirmed. "I made no secret about one of the murderers being called 'Tom,' and I told Zwieg that Armana was the one at the window."

"Hm." Otis thought about the possibilities.

"And Zwieg knew about the watch and could have warned Gordie," Jeremiah added.

"But a lot of people would have known about that watch after you nearly shot an innocent man," Otis countered angrily.

Jeremiah winced. Otis had never mentioned the incident before. Jeremiah shivered as another realization struck him, shocked him.

"There's something else, Marshal," Jeremiah went on reluctantly. "Zwieg knew about the gold shipment."

"How'd he know about that?" Otis asked.

"I told him," Jeremiah said in shame.

"What!" Otis bellowed, putting his fists on his hips. "You got a God damn big mouth, Bacon."

Jeremiah swallowed. "You think maybe—I'm responsible for Herb's death?"

"Damn right you could be," Otis agreed angrily. He sat down at his desk again, as Jeremiah buried his face in his hands.

"I feel sick," the young man said.

"Nothing you can do about it now, Bacon," Otis said gruffly. "Getting back to Zwieg, though, that's kind of interestin'."

Jeremiah looked up.

"Cyrus Kessler almost lived in that saloon," Otis related. "He drank a lot, played cards a lot, and Stacey—" Jeremiah looked taken aback. "She is a whore, you know," Otis said.

Jeremiah squirmed in his seat. "You think Zwieg could have gotten information about the gold shipments out of Kessler while he was in the saloon?"

Otis drummed his fingers on the desk. Then he ran a hand through his hair. "The man does right well for himself. The only one in town who does, matter of fact. I always thought it was just the saloon, but maybe . . ."

Jeremiah started to rise. "Let's go talk to him."

"Wait, wait," Otis cautioned. "Kessler's mouth did tend to loosen up when he'd been drinkin', but a lot of people could've heard him say something about shipments."

"Regularly?"

"That's the part that worries me." Otis thought a

moment, then shook his head. "I've known Mel Zwieg a long time. I can't believe he'd be the one."

"But it all points to him," Jeremiah argued.

"Highly circumstantial," Otis said. "It doesn't really prove anything."

"What do we do then?"

Otis swung back and forth in his swivel chair, thinking. "We know that the source of information, the brains of the gang, is right here in Point of Rocks," ne began. "But when there's a shipment of gold or greenbacks, there are still too many people who could know, somehow, about the shipments to prove one hundred percent that it was Zwieg."

"But look at—"

Otis cut him off with an upraised hand. "But suppose there's a shipment that only you, me, and Zwieg knew about."

"But that's impossible," Jeremiah stated.

"Not if it's an imaginary shipment." Otis drew his chair closer to the desk and leaned toward Jeremiah. "What if Zwieg were to *think* there was a gold shipment?" he hypothesized.

"If the stage got held up," Jeremiah said, smiling with understanding, "it would mean that Zwieg must have been the one who sent the gang."

Otis smiled and nodded. "Do you think, with your big mouth, that you can bait the trap? Say, a shipment of gold from Atlantic City coming in next Wednesday?"

Jeremiah rose quickly, chagrined at the marshal's reference to his loose lips. "You bet I can," he said eagerly.

"Here's what we'll do," Otis said. "Late Tuesday night Paul and I—and I won't even tell Paul what we're up to and don't you tell Anita. We'll ride out to South Pass City to be ready at daybreak to follow the stage from there to Point of Rocks. If the stage gets held up—"

"We come looking for Zwieg."

"And maybe chew up the gang a bit."

"Right!" Jeremiah agreed. "I'm on my way."

During the second verse of "Streets of Laredo" Zwieg wandered over to the piano. "Evening, Jeremiah," he greeted.

"Evening, Mr. Zwieg," Jeremiah said, continuing to play.

"How'd the trip go?" the saloon-keeper asked.

"Pretty good, but it'll never be the same without Herb riding along."

"No, I guess not," Zwieg agreed. "Sure hope we catch the bastard who shot him."

"Me, too," Jeremiah said grimly. "Matter of fact, I'm hoping to do just that next week."

"Next week?" Zwieg asked. "Why next week?"

"There's another gold shipment coming in Wednesday."

"So soon after the last one?"

"Yes, they're doing pretty good up there, I guess," Jeremiah said. "Oh, but keep it quiet."

"Of course."

"Anyway," Jeremiah went on, "the Red Desert Gang always seems to know when shipments are coming, so I'm going to be expecting them this time. I can't wait to get that guy in the duster under my sights."

"Watch yourself, Jeremiah," Zwieg said. "The gang has killed before; they won't hesitate to kill again."

Jeremiah considered Zwieg's statement to be a direct warning from the gang leader himself.

"Yeah, Jerry," Stacey said. "You be careful."

Jeremiah stopped playing. "Stacey," he said, surprised to see her. He looked around to see if anyone else could have overheard his talk of the gold shipment. He felt reassured.

"Don't worry, Stacey," he said, patting her on the hand. "I'm not going to do anything foolish. If it looks like they got the drop on me, I'll just let them have the gold."

"Good," Stacey said, satisfied. "I don't want anything to happen to you." She ran her fingers through Jeremiah's hair.

"Right," Zwieg put in. "We want you back playin' that piano." He turned to go. "You be careful, Jeremiah." He left and went to his office.

"Stacey," Jeremiah said. "You won't tell anyone about the gold shipment, will you?"

Stacey looked hurt. "Good heavens, no, Jerry," she said. "I want you back alive." She ran both hands through his hair.

"Stacey . . ."

CHAPTER NINETEEN

Wednesday, July 6, 1880

It was ironic that on a trip when Jeremiah was actually hoping for a holdup and a gunfight, he had picked up more passengers in Lander than he'd had all the previous week. A young couple with two small children, a cowboy, a salesman, and a merchant on a buying trip to Cheyenne.

The previous night he had mulled over the situation during dinner at the South Pass City Hotel, considering the possible consequences of gunplay around a stage full of passengers. Of course, he could make sure there was no gunplay, but the gang would then discover the ruse anyway. Would they then, in frustration and anger, turn on the passengers, robbing them, or worse?

How could he face Anita if passengers were molested and robbed or killed, particularly if such action was the result of his crusade against the Red Desert Gang?

And what of his responsibility to the passengers? Did he have the right to lead them knowingly into dangerous circumstances, if he could avoid it? He had decided that he didn't have that right.

It had taken some impassioned pleading, but Jeremiah had finally persuaded the reluctant, weary travelers to depart for Point of Rocks after only a few hours' rest in South Pass City.

They had passed through the Sweetwater River swing station in the dark, obtaining a fresh team only because Jeremiah was able to harness it himself, the manager refusing to do so until the regular time. Subsequently they had passed without incident the place where Herb had been killed. Now, the stagecoach was far south of South Pass City, and dawn was casting a growing rosiness across the eastern horizon of the Red Desert Basin to Jeremiah's left.

He felt sure they had eluded the gang and that the rest of the trip would be safe. He chuckled as he thought about the robbers waiting half the day for the stage at the ambush site.

Jeremiah urged the team to greater effort now that he could see the road better, and so it was at a fairly high speed that the stage rounded a curve and dashed through a startled group of riders, scattering them to the sides of the road.

The stage mounted a short hill, and Jeremiah looked back to investigate. Before the stage descended again and the hill blocked his view, he counted seven horses and riders milling about. He shivered involuntarily. Could that have been the Red Desert Gang, coming *up the road* to the holdup spot instead of across country?

Topping the next hill Jeremiah looked again, and his fears were confirmed. The riders were in pursuit. They were just coming over the previous hill. Jeremiah cringed as he heard shots.

As the stage sped downhill again, Jeremiah noticed the off leader falter. The horse bounced around in his harness, banged into the other leader, then staggered once, twice. Jeremiah reached for the brake, realizing that the animal had been hit.

However, before his foot touched the brake handle, the wounded animal collapsed. The other leader was yanked off his feet and somersaulted. The swing team ran straight into the fallen span, and the wheelers followed suit, all landing in a grotesque pile of horseflesh, neighing and screaming in terror and pain.

The stagecoach jackknifed, and Jeremiah was propelled through the air. He hit the ground hard and rolled helplessly through greasewood, sagebrush, and over rocks. As he rolled he heard the gut-wrenching silence as the iron tires of the stage lost contact with the ground and the nauseating crash as it landed on its side.

Jeremiah lay on the ground trying to suck air into his lungs and force his battered body to respond to his order to rise. He saw the stage horses thrashing about in a great tangle of harness and gear, wildly kicking, and screaming pitifully. From inside the coach came even more dismaying sounds: screaming, shouting, cursing, and crying.

Jeremiah finally got to his feet and stumbled toward the stage, tripping over Herb's Winchester, which had been thrown out of the boot along with everything else. His lips quivered, and his eyes watered as he surveyed the stage wreck. This was worse than what he had tried to avoid. Perhaps the marshal was right, perhaps he was trouble, drawing death and destruction to himself.

The outlaw company topped the next hill, and Jeremiah's tear-filled eyes darted their way. They were the real cause of all the trouble. If it weren't for them, he wouldn't even *be* in Point of Rocks. His father would still be alive. And Herb and Cyrus. And the passengers . . .

"You bastards!" Jeremiah screamed toward them. "You goddamn bastards!" Impulsively, he reached down and picked up the Winchester, cocked the hammer, and fired at one of the approaching, shadowy horsemen. The rider pitched backward off his horse, his pistol twirling high over his head in an arc.

Levering and firing as quickly as he could, Jeremiah put half a dozen bullets into the close-packed bunch. A horse dropped like a stone, and its rider was flung to the ground to roll about and then scurry for cover. The other riders reined in their horses, bewildered by the sudden attack that met them. They returned the fire in a heavy but inaccurate barrage of their own, as they spurred their mounts to the hills away from the road.

Jeremiah ran for some rocks he spied and crouched behind the biggest one. He pumped a few more shots at the outlaws before they found cover of their own. Ominously, only a crying child was heard from the stage, but Jeremiah hoped the others had fallen silent because of the gunfire. One of the wheelers was screaming in agony, and Jeremiah saw he'd been gored by a crosstree. A bullet into the poor beast stilled him.

By now, a more accurate gunfire was putting bullets into the rock behind which Jeremiah hid and into the dirt in front of it. Jeremiah tucked his head down and analyzed his predicament. He had a Winchester and a Colt, and the bullets in his belt fitted both. But there weren't many bullets, he was badly outnumbered, would soon be outflanked, and was stuck behind the rock. His situation was almost hopeless.

The outlaws lost no time in improving their positions. One of the gang members would make a break for a new spot, as the others poured a merciless fire on Jeremiah's position, peppering the rock with bullets. Defiantly Jeremiah fired back, even wounding one of them in the arm. But he couldn't shake the mental image of the outlaws' bullets cruelly chipping away the rock until there was nothing left of it, before they finished him off.

A sliding sound behind caught his ear, and he whirled around, Winchester ready. A carbine slid to a stop at his feet, and higher up the rise a man was rolling down, his hat veering off on a path of its own. The man came to rest at the foot of the hill, obviously dead, and Jeremiah faced forward again, amazed and puzzled.

With surprised delight he saw Otis MacKenzie wave a greeting to him from the other side of the opposite hill. The marshal's carbine appeared, and smoke burst away from its muzzle.

"I'll be damned," Jeremiah said with a growing smile. "I'll be damned." He saw another figure off to his right, firing toward the outlaws with a carbine, also. He recognized Paul Warner's hat. Jeremiah raised his Winchester and made it a three-way crossfire.

The outlaws scrambled in panic for their horses. One tumbled while he was running, another rolled off his horse right after he'd mounted and was trampled by the other horses. Three men counted themselves lucky to spur their horses into a gallop and vanish over the hill whence they had come.

Jeremiah ran from behind the rock and toward Otis, who was coming down the hill. "Man, am I glad to see you," he cried happily.

"I daresay," Otis responded.

"Hi, Paul," Jeremiah said to the deputy who joined them. He noted with satisfaction Paul's black eye.

"Yeah," Paul responded sourly.

"Bacon," Otis said, "you're a crazy fool."

"How'd you happen along?" Jeremiah asked.

"We didn't see the stage behind the blacksmith's shop when we got to South Pass City, so we roused Eldon. He said you'd already left. We rode out after you."

"I left early so I could avoid a gunfight," Jeremiah explained, breaking into a run toward the stage.

"Why?" Otis called after him.

"I've got a stage full of passengers."

"Oh, Jesus," Otis said under his breath. A man had just pushed the stage door back and was struggling to get up out of the overturned vehicle.

Incredibly, none of the passengers were killed, but there were plenty of injuries, including broken bones. Jeremiah said a prayer of thanks that it hadn't been worse.

The passengers were removed from the coach and settled alongside it. Paul tended to untangling the stage horses. He shot two more of them and predicted that another would have to be put away. Otis checked the outlaws that had been shot. He returned to Jeremiah and the passengers.

"You get that one lying out in the open there, Bacon?" he asked.

"Yes," Jeremiah answered. "When they first came over the hill."

"Well," Otis said. "That's Tom Hocker."

Jeremiah said nothing but only looked at the body. That's three, he thought.

"Two of them are still alive," Otis added, "but badly wounded. He looked up at the coach. "Will this thing run if we turn it upright?" he asked.

"I don't think so," Jeremiah said. "We sheared off a locking pin."

"Hm. Well, guess the best thing you can do for your passengers is to go to Point of Rocks and get some transportation and a doctor. Take one of the outlaw's horses."

"Okay," Jeremiah agreed. "And you?"

"I'm goin' after the three that got away. I'll leave Paul here to look after the passengers and guard the wounded prisoners."

"Okay," Jeremiah said. "And, Marshal, I'm sure glad you came along when you did. That's the second time you've saved my life."

"Bacon," Otis said, "you and Lady Luck must walk hand in hand."

CHAPTER TWENTY

Wednesday, July 6, 1880

It was early afternoon when Jeremiah raced the borrowed horse into Point of Rocks, both rider and horse thoroughly wrung out by the broiling sun. He was heading for the doctor's office and then to find Anita to arrange for a team and wagon, when he noted three well-lathered horses tied to the hitching rail of the Bitter Creek Saloon. Instantly he reined in the horse, all thought of his immediate mission evaporated.

He tied his horse to the rail and examined the other three horses and their gear. A tuft of white cloth was visible beneath the flap of one of the saddlebags. Upon lifting the flap, Jeremiah pulled out a white-linen duster. Underneath that was a sack with three holes in it. His blood rose.

Clutching the duster and hood, he strode for the front doors of the saloon and burst through. He halted, waiting for his eyes to adjust to the dim light. He heard a gravel-throated voice at the bar. The scene brightened, and he made out a man standing at the far end of the bar talking with Stacey and Zwieg in an animated conversation.

"Jeremiah!" Stacey exclaimed, seeing him.

The man in front of her twirled around and faced Jeremiah. Jeremiah held up the duster and sack. "These are yours, bastard," he said. The man stiffened, and his hand went slowly toward his holster.

The other saloon occupants scattered and ducked for cover, the men at the bar dropping their glasses and letting them spill. Zwieg grabbed Stacey by the wrist and pulled her, complaining, into his office.

"You've pushed your luck too far this time, Jeremiah Bacon," the outlaw said. "I've lost some good friends to you and the marshal."

"You killed my father," Jeremiah accused in turn, dropping the two items and pointing a finger at the man. "And you killed Cyrus Kessler and Herb Lambrecht. I'm taking you in for trial and execution. And I'm also taking in your boss, Zwieg, to hang alongside you."

"You'd have to kill me first—"

"I'm willing to oblige."

"—but I'm gonna kill you instead," the man sneered. He went for his gun.

All the marshal had taught Jeremiah, all the practicing he'd done, all his concentration and determination were now put to the test. Jeremiah's hand closed around the butt of his Colt, and he tore it out of the holster, cocking the hammer as it emerged. Both guns roared, and billows of smoke leaped for each other. Jeremiah froze with his finger still pressing the trigger against the guard, and he watched with deep satisfaction as his enemy let his pistol twirl on his trigger finger and then let it fall to the floor. The man dropped to his knees and then fell on his face, hands outstretched to the side.

That's four, Jeremiah thought triumphantly. A movement at the side of the saloon reminded him that there were three horses outside. He lurched aside. His luck held, and the first shot fired at him tore a gash in his vest but left him unscathed.

Jeremiah saw his attacker firing from behind a table, and he returned the fire immediately, his bullet tearing a chunk out of the table. The man ducked back out of sight, and Jeremiah dove for the end of the bar, wondering where the third man was.

Jeremiah looked at the patrons cowering under

tables and behind chairs. "Everybody out!" he shouted. "I won't shoot."

There was a stampede for the door, even Jason coming from behind the bar and rushing past Jeremiah. Some people left by the front door and some by the back. From his vantage point, Jeremiah noticed a pair of boots swerve from their course and head for him. He threw himself backward just as the wearer reached the end of the bar and fired at Jeremiah's former position. Jeremiah returned the fire, and his two forty-four slugs knocked the man backward, stumbling, and he crashed over a chair and lay still.

A bullet tore a long sliver from the top of the bar near Jeremiah's head. He spun toward the sound of the gunshot and fired at a man who was about to duck down the rear hallway. He missed, but the man halted and scampered back.

Jeremiah was about to fire again when he noticed a pistol sneaking around the door of Zwieg's office and pointing at him. He pivoted and fired a shot at the door, puting a jagged hole in it. The pistol disappeared inside, and the door slammed shut.

Jeremiah instantly drew a bead on the man returning from the rear hallway, just as he was diving for the rear of the piano. When he pulled the trigger all he got was an impotent click. He cursed, recalling the marshal's admonition to count his shots. Hidden behind the bar, he feverishly ejected the empty cartridges from the chambers of his Colt and reloaded.

Cautiously he peered over the end of the bar. Nowhere did he see a sign of the third man; he was still behind the piano. Jeremiah rose slightly and aimed his pistol at the piano. It would be like shooting his best friend. He fired two bullets into the instrument, about where he figured a man would be crouching. The piano complained with the twanging of breaking wires and the splintering of wood.

The outlaw thumped down onto the stage, and his

gun slid across its floor. He grimaced as he held his shoulder tightly, and Jeremiah could see blood flowing from a head wound. The man continued writhing.

Jeremiah rose from his position and rushed up to the man, keeping an eye on Zwieg's door. The sound of a single shot from the office stopped him in his tracks. Had Zwieg shot Stacey?

Jeremiah got to the outlaw and dragged the man to his feet; the man complained bitterly.

"You can walk," Jeremiah said unsympathetically. "Over to the office door." He prodded the man with the barrel of his pistol, and the two of them went up to Zwieg's door. Jeremiah pushed the man against it and then with a swift kick near the doorknob, he burst the door open. The outlaw fell inward, and Jeremiah leaped in behind him, crouching, his pistol ready.

"Jerry!" Stacey cried. The saloon girl was cowering in a back corner. Zwieg was lying on the floor, his own pistol nearby.

"You all right, Stacey?" Jeremiah asked.

"Yes," Stacey replied, "but—" She pointed to Zwieg.

Jeremiah pushed the outlaw against the wall to his left. "God, I thought he'd shot you, Stacey."

"He tried to kill you, Jerry," Stacey said, coming away from the corner. "I caught him off guard and tried to grab the gun away from him. We struggled and—I shot him."

Jeremiah patted her gently on the shoulder, seeing the consternation in her face. "You did right," he said. "Is he dead?"

"I don't know."

"Here," Jeremiah said, handing his gun to Stacey and nodding toward the outlaw leaning against the wall. "If he so much as sneezes, shoot him." Jeremiah went over to where Zwieg lay and knelt down. He was surprised to hear the wounded outlaw laugh.

"What's so funny, mister?" Jeremiah asked, looking up at him.

"Tell him, boss," the man said. He reached to the side and swung the door closed, though it didn't catch.

"Boss!" Jeremiah repeated, stunned by a revelation. He looked up at Stacey unbelievingly.

"You stupid, loud-mouthed son-of-a-bitch," she said to the man. "Now he knows."

"So what? You were gonna shoot him anyways, weren't you?"

Jeremiah's mouth dropped open as he stared wide-eyed at Stacey.

"He thought Zwieg was on top," Stacey said. "Didn't you hear him?"

"So? I don't see—"

"I could've gotten out of this," she snapped. "And I could've helped you. Jerry would've thought I shot Zwieg defendin' him, not because Zwieg figured out who I really was. What with the three of you chargin' in here, that God-damned husband of mine comin' right up to me in front of Zwieg, askin' for money."

"Husband?" Jeremiah was staggered.

"Yeah, you jackass," she hurled at him. "You shot my husband. I almost got you for that, but you nearly took my hand off. If I'd've done it, everyone would've blamed Zwieg, of course. And dead men can't defend themselves."

"Boss," the outlaw said. "I gotta get outa here. This arm is killin' me. And my head. Gimme some money so I can vamoose."

Stacey looked at him coldly. "And a dead man can't tell anyone who I really am."

"Boss—"

"The gang is finished," Stacey said. She pulled the trigger of Jeremiah's gun, and the blast reverberated in the small room. The outlaw's head banged against the wall. He hung there motionless for an instant, then crumpled to the floor.

"Stacey," Jeremiah said, horrified. "I can't believe—"

"You damned fool, Jerry," she said scathingly, pointing the gun at him. "Did you really think I was so taken by you?"

"You caused my father's death."

"An accident. If he hadn't looked in that window he'd be alive today."

"And Cyrus."

"Tough bastard, he was," Stacey said begrudgingly. "I had him so soused up before he went back to the office that night I figured he'd sleep for a week. Well, he didn't. Woke up, surprised the boys, and—"

"You were the source of the information for the holdups?"

"Hell, yes. Kessler would talk his head off in bed with a little liquor and lovin'. I even had the combination to the safe in the Wells Fargo office."

"And Herb," Jeremiah said bitterly. "Why Herb?"

"Couldn't get to Herb," Stacey said. "With Cyrus I got all Herb knew, too. Without Cyrus, no information at all. But I figured you'd take over the whole thing if Herb were gone. And I figured I could coax as much information out of you as I could out of Kessler."

Jeremiah was disgusted with himself. She was right; he'd seen a colossal fool.

"You warned Gordie," Jeremiah said.

"And Hocker," she said, completing the picture.

Jeremiah swallowed. "And what about me?"

"Sorry, Jerry," she said matter-of-factly. "You know all about me now. I'm gonna have to shoot you, too."

"Stacey," Jeremiah said, "you can't get away with this. They'll know," he insisted. He rose slowly to his feet.

"Will they?" Stacey posed. "Picture this. Everyone thinks Zwieg is the gang leader; they all heard you say before you were going to hang Zwieg. I'll fire a couple o' more shots in here. When people come in, I'll tell 'em you shot Zwieg. Then that guy," she said, nodding toward the outlaw on the floor, "grabbed your gun and shot you. Then I got the gun away from him and shot him. That leaves just me, innocent little me. Who would suspect a cotton-headed tart like me?"

"Stacey—"

"Sorry, Jerry," she repeated. "Time's awastin'. But I'll make it quick."

He started toward her, thinking he might get a chance to jump her, but she was alert.

"Far enough, Jerry," she said, cocking the hammer expertly.

The door was kicked open with a bang, and Stacey instinctively whirled and fired. Cyrus Kessler's Springfield carbine boomed, and Jeremiah gasped as a bullet tore through Stacey's body, exiting in the small of her back and lodging in the plaster wall behind her.

Her body twisted around, and she fell against Jeremiah, her head back, her eyes open but unseeing. Jeremiah clutched her reflexively, and his hands closed over the warm, moist patch of blood that was spreading around a ragged hole in the back of her red dress.

He stared down at her eyes, shamed by the recollection of the times he'd stared at them before, awash in dreams. He felt the warmth of her body pressed against him, her bosom, her hips, her thighs. He thought about how much he had coveted them, and about how much death and misery she had been responsible for. He felt utterly repulsed. He let the body down roughly.

Anita Kessler let the carbine fall from one hand until the butt touched the floor. Then she let go with the other hand, and the weapon slipped to the carpet with a soft, innocent clunk, as if it were regretful at the destruction it had just meted out.

Jeremiah went over to Anita and drew her into his arms, his body trembling. She clutched at him needfully.

"Is the killing over now, Jeremiah?" she asked hopefully.

"Yes, Anita," he said. "It's over."

CHAPTER TWENTY-ONE

Friday, July 29, 1880

Jeremiah tried to make out figures on the station platform, but he saw only his own reflection in the window of the passenger car; the black night outside turned the glass into a mirror. He leaned back and took out the letter from Professor Peters that had informed him of a job and financial support and urged him to come to San Francisco at once. He read it again, then put it back in his coat pocket.

He recalled the farewell he'd just been through. His mother fussing over him, straightening his tie. Her urging him to study hard and never give up music. To practice and study, study and practice. And write home once in a while.

Otis MacKenzie, gruff but friendly, unable to conceal a fondness for the young man who had adapted so well to the country—and who had helped rid the territory of the Red Desert Gang. He hadn't said anything about Jeremiah's mother, but Jeremiah felt sure he didn't have to worry about her as long as that great bear with a badge was around.

And Anita. Sweet, affectionate, beautiful, wonderful Anita. How he hated to part from the girl. He would taste that farewell kiss till he returned in a year, as he had promised.

He thought back to a night in June, when he and his father had stepped off the train at just about this time of night, to take that fatal stroll into Point of Rocks. His father would forever rest in this little town. Probably his mother would never leave either. And he was leaving his heart here.

The train jolted, and Jeremiah sensed it was moving. He waved out the window though he could see no one. The train picked up speed, and he thought to himself how differently it rode than a stagecoach.

He looked down at his hands. How much they'd gone through since that first night. Piano playing to be sure, but also card playing, and drinking, stage driving, riding, shooting, caressing a woman—and killing. They'd been bruised and battered, cut and scraped, tanned and hardened, callused and toughened.

And now they would once again be pushing down ivory keys exclusively. The piano and concerts and orchestras. So completely different from the life he was leaving behind in Point of Rocks. On the one hand the concert stage, on the other hand the Concord stage. He reflected for a moment longer as the train barreled along, already several miles away from Point of Rocks and the people he loved. Hell, who was he kidding? He sprang from his seat and reached for the emergency cord with both hands.

Dell Bestsellers

- ☐ **COMES THE BLIND FURY** by John Saul $2.75 (11428-4)
- ☐ **CLASS REUNION** by Rona Jaffe $2.75 (11408-X)
- ☐ **THE EXILES** by William Stuart Long $2.75 (12369-0)
- ☐ **THE BRONX ZOO** by Sparky Lyle and Peter Golenbock $2.50 (10764-4)
- ☐ **THE PASSING BELLS** by Phillip Rock $2.75 (16837-6)
- ☐ **TO LOVE AGAIN** by Danielle Steel $2.50 (18631-5)
- ☐ **SECOND GENERATION** by Howard Fast $2.75 (17892-4)
- ☐ **EVERGREEN** by Belva Plain $2.75 (13294-0)
- ☐ **CALIFORNIA WOMAN** by Daniel Knapp $2.50 (11035-1)
- ☐ **DAWN WIND** by Christina Savage $2.50 (11792-5)
- ☐ **REGINA'S SONG** by Sharleen Cooper Cohen $2.50 (17414-7)
- ☐ **SABRINA** by Madeleine A. Polland $2.50 (17633-6)
- ☐ **THE ADMIRAL'S DAUGHTER** by Victoria Fyodorova and Haskel Frankel $2.50 (10366-5)
- ☐ **THE LAST DECATHLON** by John Redgate $2.50 (14643-7)
- ☐ **THE PETROGRAD CONSIGNMENT** by Owen Sela $2.50 (16885-6)
- ☐ **EXCALIBUR!** by Gil Kane and John Jakes $2.50 (12291-0)
- ☐ **SHOGUN** by James Clavell $2.95 (17800-2)
- ☐ **MY MOTHER, MY SELF** by Nancy Friday $2.50 (15663-7)
- ☐ **THE IMMIGRANTS** by Howard Fast $2.75 (14175-3)

At your local bookstore or use this handy coupon for ordering:

Dell | **DELL BOOKS**
P.O. BOX 1000, PINEBROOK, N.J. 07058

Please send me the books I have checked above. I am enclosing $ _____
(please add 75¢ per copy to cover postage and handling). Send check or money
order—no cash or C.O.D.'s. Please allow up to 8 weeks for shipment.

Mr/Mrs/Miss _____

Address _____

City _____ State/Zip _____

Comes the Blind Fury

John Saul

Bestselling author of
Cry for the Strangers
and *Suffer the Children*

More than a century ago, a gentle, blind child walked the paths of Paradise Point. Then other children came, teasing and taunting her until she lost her footing on the cliff and plunged into the drowning sea.

Now, 12-year-old Michelle and her family have come to live in that same house—to escape the city pressures, to have a better life.

But the sins of the past do not die. They reach out to embrace the living. Dreams will become nightmares.

Serenity will become terror. There will be no escape.

A Dell Book $2.75   (11428-4)